Compelled

Hidden Secrets Saga, Volume 4

W.J. May

Published by WJ May Publishing, 2015.

This is a work of fiction. Similarities to real people, places, or events are entirely coincidental.

COMPELLED

First edition. June 7, 2015.

Copyright © 2015 W.J. May.

Written by W.J. May.

Also by W.J. May

Bit-Lit Series
Lost Vampire
Cost of Blood
Price of Death

Blood Red Series
Courage Runs Red
The Night Watch
Marked by Courage
Forever Night

Daughters of Darkness: Victoria's Journey
Victoria
Huntress
Coveted (A Vampire & Paranormal Romance)
Twisted

Hidden Secrets Saga
Seventh Mark - Part 1
Seventh Mark - Part 2
Marked By Destiny
Compelled
Fate's Intervention
Chosen Three

The Chronicles of Kerrigan
Rae of Hope
Dark Nebula
House of Cards
Royal Tea

Under Fire
End in Sight
Hidden Darkness
Twisted Together
Mark of Fate
Strength & Power
Last One Standing
Rae of Light

The Chronicles of Kerrigan Prequel
Christmas Before the Magic
Question the Darkness
Into the Darkness

The Hidden Secrets Saga
Seventh Mark (part 1 & 2)

The Senseless Series
Radium Halos
Radium Halos - Part 2
Nonsense

The X Files
Code X
Replica X

Standalone
Shadow of Doubt (Part 1 & 2)
Five Shades of Fantasy
Glow - A Young Adult Fantasy Sampler
Shadow of Doubt - Part 2
Four and a Half Shades of Fantasy
Full Moon
Dream Fighter

Compelled

Hidden Secrets Saga
Book IV
By
W. J. May
Copyright 2015 by W.J. May

Hidden Secrets Saga:

Download Seventh Mark part 1 For FREE
Seventh Mark part 2
Marked by Destiny
Compelled
Fate's Intervention
Chosen Three
Book Trailer:
http://www.youtube.com/watch?v=Y-_vVYC1gvo

W.J. May Info:

Website: http://www.wanitamay.yolasite.com

Facebook: https://www.facebook.com/pages/Author-WJ-May-FAN-PAGE/141170442608149

SIGN UP FOR **W.J. May's Newsletter** to find out about new releases, updates, cover reveals and even freebies!

http://eepurl.com/97aYf

Cover design by: Book Cover by Design

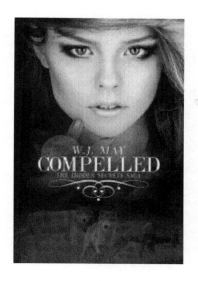

COMPELLED

Book Description

The eagerly-awaited fourth book of the Hidden Secrets Saga, Compelled continues the journey into the deliciously unique take on werewolves, witches and the living dead!

The secrets of her past have been revealed, but Rouge's life is still shrouded in mystery. Disappointed, she has found out her mother has died but learns she has a brother, who is a Grollic. It feels like she has merely scratched the surface about her life, which only creates more questions that she's driven to find answers to.

The Grollics want her dead, she's forbidden to be with the boy she loves, and her brother – who is the enemy – may be the only one she can trust. The deeper she digs into the past, the more trouble awaits.

Can she find answers in the ancient journal she carries, or is she opening Pandora's Box?

Chapter 1

I stared out the window of the Jeep as the scenery rushed by, blurs of different shades of green and brown mashed in with the pavement gray of the highway. "You killed your pack brother." The words came out slow, my brain somehow thinking if I said them at a snail's pace it might comprehend what had happened. "I thought..."

Robert turned in the seat and stared at me. "I know," he repeated. "He was going to kill you."

"I thought you were going to kill me."

My brother, who I didn't know even existed, shifted around in his seat, crossed his arms over his chest and nodded at Michael, my boyfriend. "She always this sluggish?"

Michael shrugged. "Been a bit of a crazy day."

I tapped my pointer finger against my knee, trying to remember everything Robert had told me since he'd shot his pack brother. "You killed your pack brother to protect me?"

Robert shrugged. "He's my brother—was my brother. You're my blood." He mouthed to Michael, *"What's wrong with her?"*

"Robert, you said you were the sixth. I'm the seventh. I don't know what that means."

Robert sighed. "I'm the sixth kid, you're the seventh. And my name's Rob. Only my mom called me Robert."

Rebekah was my mother too, I wanted to add but held back. She'd abandoned me. I was the seventh kid of Bentos, the marked child – the unwanted one. I leaned forward in the seat. "I'm a Grollic then? Are you sure Bentos is our father?"

Michael nearly swerved the Jeep off the road. "What the heck's going on with you, Rouge?"

Robert—Rob didn't even flinch. "Yeah. You're number seven, remember?"

I glanced at Michael, terrified he might dump both Rob and I off on the side of the road.

"You're not a Grollic, Rouge."

"No, shit!" Rob scoffed. "Neither am I, anymore." He straightened his arms and twisted in the seat again. "Can you try fixing this again? I've got nothing if I can't shift."

Michael snorted, "You should consider yourself now blessed."

The two of them looked ready to fight, and there was no way the inside of the Jeep would be enough room.

"Chill out, you two." I tried keeping my voice neutral. "Michael, since Robert—Rob can't shift, he needs protection. You said you owed him that for saving me. And—" I stared directly at Rob as I raised my voice. "If you don't want to feel like a prisoner, I suggest you stop acting like one. No one is forcing you to stay. I'll figure out how to get you to shift again if you want."

"You're going to have to," Rob said.

"She doesn't *have* to do anything," Michael growled, sounding more like the wolf than the Grollic beside him.

"She does. I have to be able to shift." Rob sighed. "She's going to need a whole army of Grollics when Bentos finds her."

Chapter 2

"What?" I knew I had yelled the word but couldn't help it.

"He's been looking for you since Mom hid you. She said you died, but he didn't believe her. That son of a bitch has been hunting you since you gave your first breath."

"How can Bentos still be alive? He should be an old, old man now."

Michael seemed infinitely patient with my constant questions. Rob, on the other hand, appeared annoyed after an hour in the Jeep with them. "Didn't we already discuss this?"

"I don't get it." My eyes darted back and forth between them. "Bentos killed Michael and his sister."

"He apparently didn't do a good job," Rob mumbled. "Dead is dead."

"Unless you're one of the twins... like I am," Michael added sarcastically.

"What I meant," I said, raising my voice. "How old is he now? What does he look like? Does the guy age?"

Rob shrugged, his eyes never leaving Michael. "He looks the same to me since I was a kid. What about you Hunter? Has your murderer changed since the last time you saw him?"

"I wouldn't know, *boy*. Last time I saw him he killed my sister right in front of me and then turned the blade on me."

"I'd like to say my heart bleeds for you, but it doesn't."

"I feel the same about your mother." Michael didn't miss a beat in his response.

The drive back to Port Coquitlam would take forever if the two of them continued on with their silly peeing contest on who was tougher, or smarter, or better, or whatever. "We get it!" I hollered. "Michael doesn't trust you, and you don't trust him. You're both only here because of me." They needed to focus on right now. "There's a mob of angry Grollics which are probably hunting us down and closing in on us because they can hear the two of you!"

"And you," both men said at the same time.

I cleared my throat. "Fine." I stared down at the journal lying on the seat beside me. I blinked rapidly trying to hold back the tears threatening to fall. My thoughts from the past while spilled out. The words came, barely a whisper, "I thought my mother had abandoned me, but she hid me to protect me. I have a brother, that's a Grollic, who's willing to fight to protect me and I just jacked up his ability to shift. My father killed my boyfriend and my best friend about a hundred years ago. They should both be dead, but instead they are alive like some vampire that doesn't need blood. That happened a long time ago and yet, my father's still alive and probably not aged a day. He's got Voodoo powers, which got passed on to me. And you think all of this is because of some stupid digit?"

"It's *the* number. Seven. Seventh Mark. Bentos is the Seventh Mark. You have it also... with more." Rob's voice held sympathy I didn't expect to hear.

"She doesn't," Michael said, cutting him off.

"She does. You haven't looked. Or you purposely avoided seeing it. You know it's there."

My shoulder burned at the mention of the mark. Somehow, I didn't want to talk about the mark here, in front of Rob. I needed to be alone with Michael. "I can't turn into a Grollic, right?"

He shook his head and then nodded. "I have no clue. Legend says you control the beast, you aren't one of us. You mingle with his kind," he said, jerking his chin toward Michael. "I have no idea what you're capable of."

"What else do you know about Rouge?" Michael passed a slow moving car and continued pushing the Jeep past the speed limit.

"She's right about the number. Except it's not just seven."

"What do you mean?" I asked, picking up the journal and trying to draw strength from it. It seemed to work.

"You draw your ability as the seventh child, but you also have the strength of three."

I had no idea what he meant. "Pardon?" I stared at Michael through the rear-view mirror. "Do you what that is?"

"I don't know, Rouge."

Rob set his seat back and settled in for the ride. "Why'd you pick Rouge instead of Jamie, by the way? Or did you not even know your name is Jamie?"

"I didn't. Rouge was on my foster papers and whatever mangy bits of identification were left for me. It's spelled R-O-U-G-E."

Rob harrumphed. "Like the French spelling for red." He leaned his head back and closed his eyes. "Like a damn fairy tale; Red Riding Hood and the big bad wolf, and, of course, all the sevens and threes. It's ridiculous and ironic."

"Big words from a boy who lived in the crap end of town." I set the journal open on my lap. "Don't forget the witch part. I'm apparently carrying Bentos' spell book."

"You are so going to get me killed." Rob tried to sound annoyed, but I caught the corners of his mouth twitching upward. He wanted this. He wanted to finally have the chance to go after Bentos.

"What do you mean by the strength of three?"

Rob opened one eye and looked at Michael. "You haven't told her?"

Again, my head bobbed back and forth like watching a tennis game. "Why would Michael know?" I leaned forward again. "You two act like you hate each other one moment, and the next it's like you've known each other a long time."

Rob harrumphed and closed his eyes. He pulled his baseball hat out of his back pocket and stuck it on top of his face. "I don't know Michael personally. I know his kind though and he's with the crap-master Caleb. Mikey knows a shitload more than he's telling you. Maybe you should ask him what's going on first, then lay into me." He yawned from under the hat. "I'm going to sleep. I haven't had any since the freakin' day you showed up at my place."

I stared at the brother I didn't know I had. My gut told me to trust him. These days, following it seemed the smartest thing to do. "What's going on Michael?"

"Nothing." He kept his eyes on the road in front of him.

"What aren't you telling me?"

"I'm not hiding anything." He swallowed and I watched his Adam's apple disappear and pop back up again on his beautiful, strong neck. "I'm not concealing anything more than you are."

It was a loaded statement. He knew I was hiding something too. Michael said he knew more than me; I knew more than what I had told him and Robert knew more than any of us. I chose to ignore Michael's comment. I would not argue with him today, especially with Robert in the Jeep with us.

At one point, all three of us would have to stop arguing and start sharing. Or none of us would stop Bentos. We were going to need the three of us, and a whole army of Grollics and Hunters to stop the bastard.

"If Bentos is still alive and hunting me down, why hasn't he found me yet?" I had a million questions. I pulled out the journal I had bought to write in and began jotting everything down on the first blank page I came across. These questions were all going to need answers.

Michael pressed his lips together and then forced air through his nose. "I don't know."

Rob snorted again from under his hat. His lack of belief was growing annoying. "It's because you didn't have your power yet.

When you turned eighteen, he upped his search for you. He could feel you alive. When you used your ability the first time, he felt his strength weaken. Every time you learn to control your gift, he's going to lose some control of his."

"Seriously?"

"I'm supposed to be sleeping. You two are theoretically supposed to be hashing this out." Rob sighed. "Only in my dreams." He sat up and stuffed his hat on top of his head.

I watched him. He was very handsome. I could see some similar lines and curves on his face that were similar to mine. The hair seemed to be the biggest giveaway. I smiled. I had a brother.

"Bentos can sense you now. You have the ability so when he comes back to Niagara Falls, which he will, he's going to know you were there. I had to kill Marcus because of that also."

"What?" I pictured Marcus, his shirt suddenly filling with blood.

"If we left him alive, Bentos would drill him for answers." Rob sighed. "You can't question the dead, they don't know how to lie – or be forced to tell the truth."

I hated myself for having Rob choose between what he had and someone he barely knew, me. "When this is all over, you'll be able to go back and explain to your pack what happened." This was my fault, because of me he was now on the run.

Rob stared out the side window and didn't say anything.

"He can't go back, Rouge," Michael said calmly, as if he didn't really care.

"Why not?"

"He went against his pack. He killed a brother. That's not exactly something a pack of Grollics will forgive and welcome you back with open arms."

"He's their Alpha. He can explain to them—"

"Explain to them what?" Rob snapped. "That I chose you, over them? You're the enemy, Jamie. You're the one we want dead – more than the Hunters." He waved his hand. "You,

Bentos, all the sevens are atrocities. Freaks from the bowels of hell." He made an effort to lower his voice, but it didn't work. "Sorry." It didn't sound like he meant it.

"For what?" I imagined all the things Bentos had done that I didn't know about and it made me sick to my stomach. "I'm not my father. You saved my life." *A debt must be repaid.* I straightened. Where had those words come from? I hadn't thought them, but I knew I believed them. He had saved my life. I owed him the same in return. I stared idly at the journal. There was no honor in the ability I had. It was a curse.

"I saved your life and in doing so, destroyed my own." Rob pressed his lips tight together. "I didn't do this for you. I did this for Rebekah. She would have wanted it." He punched his knee. "I never should have stayed in that stupid apartment waiting for you to come by one day. Never knowing if you actually would. When your birthday came and passed this January and you didn't show, I thought..." He shook his head. "It doesn't matter."

"Did Bentos come looking for Rouge on her birthday?" Michael sped along the highway, paying no heed to the signs posted on how fast he was supposed to travel.

"He showed up in December, instructed us to contact him immediately if she showed up. He came again in January a few days before your birth date and left a week after. Killed five of my pack." Rob paused a moment, apparently remembering it was no longer his pack. "He commanded more shit when you didn't show up and took off to Florida when a pack of Grollics down there were annihilated. Was that you?"

I shook my head and didn't miss Michael's warning look in the rear-view mirror. He didn't want me to say anything about what had happened in Port Coquitlam. I'd decimated the entire pack with a few words and no one knew about it. Not one of them had survived. All the evidence lay buried in the bottom of the lake. "I've never been to Florida."

"Then where have you been the past fifteen years?"

Michael held up his hand. "Don't answer him, Rouge."

"She can tell me whatever she wants. I'm her brother." Rob scowled at Michael. "Is he always this bossy to you?"

"He's—"

Michael cut me off. "She doesn't know if she can trust you! You *just* told us that Bentos had been in Niagara Falls looking for her, commanding you to inform him when she showed up."

He had a point. A very good one. Rob could have gone into that shop in Grand Island and contacted Bentos. Told him what we were driving and what direction we would be heading. Had we told him yet we were on the west coast? I couldn't remember. Annoyed and ticked, more at myself for being so gullible, I lifted my chin and stared down my nose at the guy who was supposed to be my brother. "Where's Bentos?"

The Jeep swerved as Michael jerked his head to turn and look at me, his eyes wide.

Rob didn't even bat an eye. "I don't know. Last time I saw him was February. He's going to find you. It's inevitable."

"Why? Are you going to tell him where I am because he forced you to?"

"No."

"Did he command you to tell him?"

"He did."

"Then how do you contact him?" I felt anger burning deep inside of me. I wanted the stupid Grollic in front of me dead. Two words from me and he could be gone forever.

"You don't. He'll come back to town and force you to tell him. Like you're doing now."

What? "I'm not forcing you to do anything." I heard myself snarl the words but didn't believe they'd come from me.

"Rouge?" Michael said softly.

I looked at him and realized he'd pulled the Jeep over to the side of the curb.

"What're you doing?" Michael kept his voice calm and measured. It sounded strange that he would talk to me like that.

When had we stopped? I glanced around and then at Rob. I could feel my eyes grow wide.

"What did you just say to Rob?" Michael's face and voice remained calm, but the way he gripped the steering wheel warned me he wasn't. He seemed... scared.

"W-What do you mean?" Suddenly I knew the answer and cringed. I'd done it again! Spoken in the stupid language. I stared down at the tight fists I'd curled my hands into, now resting on my thighs. "I'm sorry, Rob. I didn't realize..." My voice trailed off.

Rob blinked a few times and then shuddered. "I freakin' hate that!" He punched the dashboard. "Why the hell did you pull that crap on me? I'm not going to lie to you!" He glared, beyond furious, his eyes molting to yellow and remaining that eerie color. His body was fighting the control I'd put him under to not change.

Anger coiled inside of me. The urge to fight back stronger than I had ever felt, even against Damon. "I barely know you! Maybe I needed to be sure."

"Sure of what?"

"That you're not going to rat me out!" Cars zoomed by on the left side of the Jeep, shaking the Jeep from the wind impact. I didn't care. "Let me out," I commanded, my voice low and hateful. I knew I was controlling Rob again, using my witch-controlling magic. "Now."

Michael reached to stop Rob as he reached and pulled the door handle. He was out and pushing the seat forward so I could get out.

I scrambled out fast, knowing Michael wanted to keep driving and get away from this devil's pit. I hopped over the small road barrier and ran to the farming field beside the highway. Rob followed, close on my heels.

"You," he hissed, "are just like your father." He spat on the ground. I spun around, ready to make him peel his own skin from his flesh.

He collided into me, unable to stop in time. His was bigger than I realized, and a lot stronger. I went flying backward, arms and legs flapping in the air as I tried to catch myself. I landed on my back, knocking the wind out of my lungs.

Rob squatted down, not offering his hand to help me up but glaring down at me with his yellow, hazel eyes. "I can't believe my mother died protecting you!"

The words hurt more than I thought they would. The uncontrolled anger I had felt a moment ago evaporated as disappointment flooded my insides. I dropped my head back against the dried soil and closed my eyes. Tears escaped the sides and raced down. "I never asked for any of this," I whispered.

"No. You didn't." Rob's voice held no sympathy. "Neither did I. And I highly doubt your freak of a boyfriend did either. But we all have our own crap to deal with. So start dealing with it."

I felt Michael stand beside me and I opened my eyes to look up at the two men staring down at me. Michael's bright blue eyes kept riveting back and forth between me and Rob. I sucked in air, trying to catch my breath back.

Michael's mouth shifted to a thin, tight line. "If you *ever* touch her again—"

"I didn't!" Rob threw his hands up in the air. "She stopped running!"

Michael stepped over me as Rob took a step back. "Bull—"

"Stop it!" I hissed. "Shut up, both of you."

The tone of my voice made them both hesitate and turn to me.

Rob shifted. "What—"

I sat up, holding a hand in the air to quiet him before pointing in the opposite direction of where the Jeep and the highway were.

Both guys' heads swivelled in the direction of my finger.

"You have got to be joking," Michael muttered.
"Change me back *now*," Rob demanded.

Chapter 3

"Grollics?" I squinted across the farm field into the dense forest beyond. "Already?" I scrambled up and started running for the car. "How'd they catch us so fast?"

Neither Michael nor Rob responded. They weren't ahead of me like I expected. I skidded to a stop.

Michael stood, casual but his legs set shoulder-width apart and ready to fight.

Rob squatted, one hand on the ground like a football player in a three-point stance.

They were going to fight, not run.

"Crap," I muttered and reached for my bag, realizing I didn't have it on me. *Protect the journal.* What if more Grollics surrounded the Jeep and found it? I didn't understand everything inside the wolf book, but allowing it to fall into the hands of a Grollic was something I could not risk happening.

Dirt flickered under my shoes as I raced for the Jeep. I could hear the beating of running, like horses galloping, behind me with the sound of growling and snapping of teeth. I threw my right hand out behind me. "Change, Rob. Please, change."

Just before hopping over the guard rail I glanced back. There had to be at least a dozen Grollics halfway across the field. The beasts' bright amber eyes reflected brightly against the setting sun. Their large, grotesque mouths and elongated noses flashed, all teeth and saliva. They were massive creatures with muscles that rippled as they raced toward Michael and Rob. Their greasy matted hair shivered against the dark leather of their skin. *The same color as my journal.*

I leapt over the guard rail and rushed to the Jeep. Thankfully no demonized animal stood waiting for me anywhere near the vehicle. They must've been chasing us and now, because we'd stopped, had managed to catch up.

"Give me enough time to get my book. Just hold till I get back there," I whispered as I grabbed the door handle and then jerked the seat forward. My blood forgot to flow as time seemed to stop.

The journal lay on the seat, oblivious to the war about to break out behind me.

"Is there a problem, miss?"

I jumped and banged my head as I pulled myself out of the back seat of the Jeep. Slipping the journal under my shirt I spun around, ready to hoof the person behind me.

A middle-aged man in a dark blue one-piece outfit stood a safe distance away. His name was sewn into his suit, Lenny. His tow truck sat parked behind the Jeep with his hazards flashing. Definitely not a Grollic.

"Oh! No, I'm f-fine," I said, rushing the words out. "Just trying to get something from the back seat."

A large growl erupted in the field making both of us jump. Lenny glanced over and quickly back to me. "That didn't sound normal."

I forced a laugh, wishing he would just jump back in his truck and leave. "Yeah, kind of creepy." I held my arms over my stomach, trying to hide the journal that seemed to be growing warmer against my skin. "We should probably get out of here."

Lenny didn't take the hint. "I read on the Internet the other day there are some wild animals that they have no record of before. Big cat-like beasts, like black panthers. Here in New York." He glanced at the Jeep's license plate. "You're not from around here? You all by yourself?"

Goosebumps rose on my arms and back. The attack in the field was seconds away from happening. If one of those beasts got past Michael or Rob, they would come after me, and Lenny was a sitting duck out here in the open.

A painful yowl erupted into the air. The setting sun had darkened the field and the small tree line hid part of the field from sight. You could see Michael and Rob from where the Jeep sat.

Lenny moved toward the guard rail. "Something's been hurt. Two animals must be fighting." He hesitated before stepping over. "Maybe..."

"You shouldn't go over there." I exhaled a breath I didn't know I'd been holding.

"Not without my gun." He hurried back to his truck.

Not good. The idiot was going to get himself killed and possibly me or Rob in the process. Michael might have the ability to prevent death, but Rob and I didn't stand a chance. I leapt over the railing and sprinted past the tree line to the fields.

Rob hadn't shifted. He stood in nearly the same position as when I had taken off a moment earlier.

Michael on the other hand moved in a blur. Three Grollics lay dead on the ground, four more not far from him. There were more beasts further away in the field.

I blinked and tried to figure out what the heck was going on. Michael slashed the throat of the Grollic nearest to him and it fell to the ground as it bled out. He moved to the next one.

It was then I realized the Grollics were not moving, as if they were frozen.

"Stop Michael!" I screamed. Something wasn't right. Why weren't they attacking? I pulled the journal out from under my shirt, the heat from it almost burning me now.

"Release me," Rob hissed.

"What?" I glanced frantically at him before looking back at Michael who stood posed, knife in the air, ready to kill the next frozen Grollic.

"You've done your Voodoo thing and halted all of them—us, even I can't move. What the hell did you do... again?"

I took a deep breath, and ran through my actions the past while. "I was trying to get you to shift again. Then I mumbled something while I went to grab the book." My mouth dropped as I remembered. Tow-truck Lenny would be pushing his way through the trees soon, ready to shoot everyone once he saw the beasts. Somehow the Grollics had become frozen because I'd said something. I couldn't even remember if I'd said anything out loud, but they'd heard it. Maybe when I was close to the journal I had extra Voodoo. Could the book give me more power? "Ok. Whatever. You unfreeze." I pointed at Rob and flicked my wrist. "Just you. Not the others."

He nodded and straightened immediately before rushing over to Michael, ready to kill the beast in front of him.

"Wait!" I ran as fast as I could to catch up. "There's got to be another way." I reached for Michael's arm still in the air. "We don't have to kill them!" The journal burned my hand, as if angered by my words. I forced myself to ignore the searing pain. "Change!" I hissed. "Shift back to human. Don't EVER again shift into Grollic. Wait!" Another thought hit me. "Before you change, I want—I command—you to be unable to remember you were ever here. Forget me. Forget Michael. Forget Rob, he's not your pack. Go home and leave us alone. Even Bentos will not get the truth from you."

I glanced at Rob, afraid I might send the same damning spell on him.

He stood, mouth hanging open and eyes wide as he watched me and then slowly turned to the beasts around him.

I exhaled. He didn't appear affected. Maybe because he hadn't shifted to Grollic form. I couldn't be sure because it seemed like he'd understood what I had said.

He jumped back at the same time Michael did. Michael grabbed me and half carried-half dragged me with him as he moved.

Suddenly the air quivered with invisible static. The Grollic closest to us glared, his eyes narrowing in his large head, turning from yellow to a dark red, almost black in color. His face contorted and the oily leathered body began to take on a new shape and lighten in color. The snarl shrunk as his massive canine teeth disappeared. I couldn't stop myself from staring. The kyphosis back arched and straightened as his chest returned to normal human size. The anger in his eyes turned to fear. Behind him, the other remaining Grollics went through the same process.

"What the hell?"

Michael spun around and stood in front of me at the sound of tow-truck Lenny's voice. He raised the blade in his hand, ready to attack.

The now-human Grollics turned and raced back toward the forest, their bare bottoms white against the last remaining bits of light.

Rob was the first to react. "I got it!" He waved his phone in the air as I stared stupidly at him, pretty sure Michael had the same look on his face that I did. "Wait till drama class sees our skit! No one's going to top that."

Lenny lowered the rifle he had aimed at the forest. "This some kind of prank?" He shook his head, probably ready to turn the gun on any of us.

I stepped forward and forced a laugh out again. "Yeah. I couldn't tell you up by the Jeep. So sorry about that. We all, uh, have microphones on." I purposely turned to Michael. "Did you get everything?"

He nodded, the first time in my life I'd seen him unable to react quickly.

"What about them?" Lenny pointed the tip of his gun at the four dead Grollics on the ground.

Thankfully he didn't go near them.

"Props." Rob walked over to one and lifted up an ugly clawed foot. "Seriously disgusting 'eh?"

Lenny shook his head. "What the heck are they teaching you in school these days?" He tipped his hat. "Get your Jeep off the side of the highway. If a cop comes by, he'll arrest all of you for being out here and leaving the vehicle unattended. Does the farmer who owns these fields know you're here? If not, he's going to be ticked as well." He shook his head as he rubbed his chest. "You people are nuts." He began walking back in the direction of the highway and then stopped and turned around. "What's the name of your skit?"

"Huh?" Rob's eyebrows squashed together.

"You know, the name of your movie thing. In case it goes viral. I can tell people I nearly messed it all up." He chuckled.

"We haven't come up with a title yet."

Lenny nodded, his face completely serious. "You know that song; 'If you go down to the woods today, you're sure of a big surprise.' That would be perfect as the background music during the credits."

I giggled. This was freakin' ridiculous. There were dead Grollics right beside the guy and he was singing that song? I covered my mouth, trying to stop the snickering. "Thanks."

He waved and turned back toward the highway again, this time whistling the tune to the song he'd just sang.

We watched his truck lights pull back onto the highway and disappear from sight.

"Now what?" I asked. The journal in my hand no longer held its incinerating heat. I stared at it, completely baffled by everything.

"We go." Rob shivered and set his shoulders back. "Let's get the hell out of here."

"We bury the bodies first." Michael grabbed one of the dead Grollic's massive legs and began dragging it.

"We don't have time." Rob crossed his arms over his chest, refusing to help.

"We don't have a choice. If these things shift back into human, someone's going to report a murder, and tow-truck Lenny's going to tell the police about us."

"They aren't going to shift," Rob mumbled, but grabbed another dead Grollic and followed Michael toward the tree line closer to the highway.

"How do you know they won't shift?" Michael dragged the dead thing as its head bumped against the ground, its dead eyes staring at nothing and its tongue covered in dirt and blood. "I've seen your kind shift after death."

I followed along, checking the road for any police or other drivers who might stop to check if everything was all right. Even as I watched, I didn't miss the disgusted look Rob shot Michael. "Did you not listen to what your girlfriend said to them?"

Michael dropped the dead beast and stepped over it, kicking it hard down the small slope toward a ravine. It managed to roll down without hitting any trees. Other animals would feast tonight on its remains. By the time anyone found it, they wouldn't be able to recognize what it was. "I couldn't understand what she was saying."

"She hasn't translated the thing for you yet?" Rob pulled his Grollic body down the hill and set it further away from the other body, and hidden behind a bunch of pine trees.

Michael stood beside me, glaring at my brother. "I'm going to kill him before we get home. I'm saying sorry now so I don't have to when it happens."

"I can hear you!" Rob called from the base of the ravine.

Michael huffed and went to go grab the two remaining Grollics. I turned to go with him.

"Just get in the Jeep, Rouge. The sooner we get out of here, the better." He sighed and moved into the dark field.

Rob scrambled up the hill. "Your boyfriend's an idiot."

"So are you!" I stomped away and headed back to the Jeep. I angrily wiped the tears from my eyes, blaming them on frustration and the shock from what had just happened.

They were still arguing when they got back into the Jeep where I sat impatiently waiting. I'd tucked the Grollic journal back into my knapsack beside the diary I had bought to keep notes in. Michael zoomed onto the quiet stretch of highway as he and Rob continued to disagree.

I pulled my journal out, along with a pen. Maybe writing in it would calm me down and distract me from them. After a few paragraphs I slammed the book shut. "Can you guys put a cork in it? I saved both your asses."

Their arguing went into an anaphylactic shock for a moment.

"You did not," they both said at the same time.

"Whatever. You both would have been annihilated if I hadn't stopped the Grollics. I made it easy for you."

"We could have taken them." Michael straightened in his seat.

"I could have easily done it on my own," Rob added.

"Shut it! Both of you!" I laughed at the irony. We could have been killed, or worse, caught by Bentos, and these two were fighting about a girl helping them? I leaned forward, suddenly giddy when I should be in shock. It amazed me how calm and relaxed I felt... almost cocky. "Admit it, you need me. You both do." *And you need each other right now.*

Michael caught my gaze as a passing car's headlights lit the inside of our Jeep for a split second. "You're still learning what abilities you have. You don't know all of what you can all do. I don't know what you said tonight, but I'm not sure about the men who left. We should have killed them all."

"They won't tell," I tried to explain. "I told them not to. They won't even remember us. If Bentos shows up asking questions, he wouldn't get any answers."

"What did you say to them?" Michael pressed.

"Told them to forget about us. All three of us."

Michael exhaled slowly, always the infinitely patient one with me. "I don't know if simple words are strong enough."

"They will be. I'm the one who said them." I didn't know how to make Michael understand. I barely understood it myself.

Rob snorted and shifted in his seat. "Bentos may still be able to get information from them. He knows their faces, even in human form."

"Bentos can undo what I've done?" It didn't seem possible.

"Rouge, you have his journal. How do you not know?" Rob's eyebrows rose high on his forehead.

How much did I tell him? How much did Rob already know? I glanced at Michael for confirmation.

He nodded, his lips pressed in a thin line.

"I can't read all of the journal. Only parts of it."

Rob groaned as he stuffed his hat on backwards on his head. "We're so screwed! Bentos still holds his power, even if you are able to absorb some of it, he's still stronger than you, probably stronger than all of us put together."

"Maybe he won't come looking for me."

"He's going to find you. You need to stop pretending and start preparing," Rob replied without missing a beat of the conversation.

"What do you mean?" I glanced behind me, half expecting to see a new pack of Grollics racing to take the Jeep down. "I don't have some honing beacon or something inside of me do I?"

Rob rolled his eyes and muttered something about being in a car with a bunch of idiots.

I decided ignoring it was probably better than asking what he meant. A yawn escaped from my lips. "Is it going to be safe to stop somewhere tonight?"

"We won't be stopping for a while. Maybe try and get comfortable, we're going to be taking a long detour ride home." Michael reached behind his seat and patted my knee. "I'll make sure we've got somewhere safe to rest."

Safe? That word almost sounded foreign at the moment. Nowhere seemed to be safe. We drove in silence, all of us exhausted and probably worried about what was to come. I had a brother who didn't want to be here, a father who wanted me dead and a mother who was already gone. Since meeting Michael, part of me had wanted so badly to be like him. It would never happen. I was the daughter of his worst enemy. I'd been shocked last year to learn who I was, but things just seemed to be getting more and more complicated. Michael and I weren't going to work. We would never be allowed. We both knew it. Just neither of us could admit it out loud.

I leaned forward, wanting some answers from my so-called brother and trying to forget about what was inevitably going to happen. "What did you mean before," I asked, "when you said Bentos is stronger than me? I assumed he was but I thought..." I wasn't sure how to word everything without sounding like an idiot.

"You probably don't understand any of this." Rob glared at Michael. "Because someone's never filled you in."

"She needs to find things out for herself." Michael's eyes grew bright blue. "It's not my, or your, place to tell her everything."

"And it's not your place to hide it. You and your precious – what's his name again – Caleb? You're his understudy; you're never going to go against him, or your ridiculous hierarchy. You do know he's just using her as a pawn in your games to get rid of us Grollics."

"I can just drop you off here." Michael's voice took on a tone that sent a shiver through me. "I won't even bother stopping the car. Just open the door."

"And leave her to be part of your shit? Wouldn't you love that?"

"Stop it!" I said.

"I'm using her? What's the sudden interest in *your* long-lost sister? Doesn't seem you were looking very hard for her the past fifteen years." Michael pushed the accelerator as he grew angrier. "What're your plans? Sacrifice her to Bentos so he loves you and gives you a seat on the left side of his throne?"

"Stop it, please," I repeated to both of them.

"Why are you with a *Hunter*?" Rob threw the question at me before turning back to Michael. His eyes changed color, but thankfully he didn't shift. I wasn't sure I had fixed his ability. "And what about you, precious Michael? You do realize she's a nightmare dressed up like a day dream? She's not yours, with or without that stupid necklace."

"Shut up!" I screamed and then lowered my voice. "Whatever you guys think of each other, or of me, it needs to stop." When both of them opened their mouth to protest, I continued before either had a chance to speak. "At this moment, we only have each other. Quit trying to see who is bigger, tougher or better. You're going to end up killing each other. Just leave it alone for tonight. Please, Michael."

Rob huffed. "Pretty boy here with the ocean blue eyes is lucky I'm not going to change into a Grollic inside this tiny heap and kill my sister." He glared at Michael and sneered, "You're the first guy I've met who gets his girlfriend to fight his battles."

"Enough!" I slapped the back of Rob's head, sending the cap flying. "He will kill you, and I'm not going to stop Michael if he does."

Chapter 4

Beyond exhausted, I fell asleep in the back of the Jeep and woke some time later with no clue what time it was or where we were. Sitting up, I yawned and listened to Rob's growl of a snore repeat as he inhaled again and again. "That's annoying," I muttered.

"Try listening to it for the past two hours." Michael chuckled, hearing me clearly.

"Where are we?"

"West Virginia."

"What?" I glanced out the unlit windows trying to see into the darkness. There were no street lights as we drove, just the high beams of the Jeep telling Michael where to go. "Where are we going?"

"Caleb's got a place in Beckley. It's a small safe house but no one will find us there. We need to change vehicles, stock up on weapons and get organized. I can contact him from there also."

"What are we doing?"

"Driving to Virginia."

I poked his shoulder, my other hand reaching for the Siorghra necklace around my throat. "I know that. I meant, what's the plan? We going to run and hide?"

"No!" Michael glanced at Rob when he snorted and then shifted, a moment later the steady snore returned. "I'm not exactly sure what we will do. I know what we *aren't* going to do, and that's hide. I'm not running or hiding."

"So you want to face Bentos head on?" My voice sounded so calm and yet everything inside me shook with fear. "I'm not ready to battle him."

"You will be when the time comes."

What did he know that he wasn't telling me? I stared out the front window at the weaving road in front of us. We were making a slow and steady climb uphill. "Where do we go after Beckley?"

"Grace is meeting us there. We'll wait for her and then head south. Maybe Florida. Rob seems to think Bentos was there looking for you and cleared out a pack of Grollics. Might be the least likely spot he would look. The Niagara Falls pack is going to remember the Jeep or our license plate. They'll know we are from the west coast and it won't be hard to track us."

I'd forgotten for a moment that he could communicate with Grace like a two-way radio inside their heads.

"I haven't told her everything," he added. "She'll tell Caleb. He needs to stay in Port Coquitlam in case Bentos shows up there."

"What aren't you telling me?" I didn't want to argue with Michael, but Rob had made some valid comments. We all had secrets. Michael seemed to have more and more these days.

"I don't know what you mean." Michael kept his tone neutral.

"Why would Caleb come here? What didn't you tell Grace?" I knew my voice had risen but I didn't care at this point. I was tired of information that didn't answer all my questions.

"Rob." Michael drove around a sharp bend and turned the fog lights on to give better light. He had excellent night vision so I wasn't sure why he would do it, or maybe it was just a natural human habit.

One word? That was it? "What about him? You angry because he knows things about you, and you don't know anything about him?"

"No!"

"Really? Because the two of you seem to be trying to fight over who's tougher, and stronger and better to protect me. I don't need either of your protection if that's how you guys are going to be. You'll be more of a danger than a help. I—"

"Rouge," Michael cut me off. "I didn't tell Grace about Rob because if Caleb found out he would come down here and kill him. Or take him away to experiment on him. He won't care he's your brother. A Grollic is a Grollic."

"Oh." My lips stayed in the 'O' shape as I wondered how I'd let my mouth run off again. "So Grace doesn't know about Rob?"

He shook his head. "We didn't know you had any family."

"What if there are more? Rob said he was sixth and I'm seventh. There are five more out there."

Michael shook his head. "I doubt it. I'm guessing Bentos has killed them off." He hesitated before quietly adding, "Or we have."

"Pardon?" My head turned sharply.

"Caleb's been around a long time. He knows a lot of stuff."

"I don't give a crap what he knows. What do *you* know?" It bothered me that Rob had said Michael knew things he wasn't telling me. How long had he been holding things back? He loved me. I was certain because he had given me his Siorghra. It was his life beat, his heart sitting close to mine. He was a Hunter. They didn't give that to just anyone.

"I know Rob doesn't have any other siblings before him. They are all dead. Caleb killed them."

"All of them?"

"The ones he could find. Some were dead before he found them. According to Caleb, six were dead. He must've got one wrong."

I couldn't believe Michael had never told me this before. It also made sense why he didn't believe Rob or never thought I might have family. "How would Caleb know he had one of Bentos' children?"

"It isn't as impossible as it sounds. Caleb was a born Hunter. One of the other Elders from the Higher Coven once told me that Caleb used to be incredibly patient. It's changed over time but he no longer hunts, he leads." Michael sighed, the weight of being Caleb's understudy probably sat heavy on his shoulders at times. "One of the earlier remains he thought was Bentos' offspring might have been a relation to Bentos. Possibly a cousin or uncle or something, I'm not exactly sure. These days blood work and DNA helps a ton. Caleb," he corrected himself, "we, didn't know about Rob. We thought the sixth son had been found. That's why I never thought, never considered, Rob might be your brother. It just didn't seem possible. Hunting for the seventh, you, we were looking for a son. We—I—never expected to find a girl... or fall in love with her."

"You were hunting me?" This is what Rob must've known. "And Rob?"

"We weren't hunting Rob."

I dropped back against my seat, crossing my arms over my chest. "Of course not, you thought the sixth son was already dead." I was mad. Beyond furious. I'd never been mad at Michael before but the anger inside felt like the ball of hatred I felt toward Grollics. I tried to focus on breathing to control the fury. When I was mad like this, I had a habit of controlling Grollics with a language I didn't even understand how it worked. *Vargulf Bentos Monstrums.* I was the one who made the monsters my servants. What if I lashed out in anger? I could say something and not mean it, like have Rob bite Michael. It would kill him. The thought terrified me.

Enough to lessen the anger so I could control it. "Why do you hunt us?"

They had driven into some sort of small town with stop lights now appearing on the highway. A sign showed Beckley not far off. Michael sighed as he pulled into the left lane and slowed the Jeep. "Us? You're not one of them, Rouge."

"How do you know that?" The familiar burn stung near my shoulder blade. "Answer the freakin' question. Why are you hunting Bentos' children?"

"I'm not sure." He turned at the second light and headed down another dark lit road. The sun would be rising soon and the sky had turned the predawn grayish color.

"Caleb knows why. So do you, don't lie." *You're his freakin' understudy. Of course you know why!!*

"I follow orders."

"Follow orders?" The volume of my voice had Rob jumping forward.

His eyes burned yellow as he glanced groggily between Michael and I. "Oh, crap," he muttered before settling back against his seat and closing his eyes tight.

"You're not a soldier. Caleb isn't Bentos. He doesn't control you." My words came out tight, each word sharp and enunciated. "Why kill *them?*"

Michael didn't miss the way I said *them*. "I don't think this is the time to discuss this." He glanced toward Rob.

"You think he's going to rat you out?" I was yelling and I didn't care. "He's admitted who he is. He hasn't run from you, or tried to kill you when the Grollics attacked before! I'm starting to think he's the only one who's actually on my side."

Michael pulled down a gravel and dirt road before pulling into a driveway that led to an old farm house. He drove the Jeep toward the large, paint-peeling red barn behind the house, up on the hill. It looked like a dump. He put the car in neutral. "It's pretty complicated, Rouge." He jumped out and slid aside an old painted American wood flag picture on the barn wall beside the main door. Inside lay a keyless remote entry. He punched in a code and silently made his way back to the Jeep as the barn doors opened.

Thankfully Rob stayed quiet. He had sat up and silently watched Michael.

Michael sat back in the Jeep and drove it inside the barn.

What looked like a dump outside changed instantly inside. The barn lights lit as the Jeep drove past sensors. The place looked like an underground garage.

"Holy shit, Batman," Rob said, ducking his head to look at the second floor. "It's like the Bat-Cave."

Different trucks and large vehicles lined the one side of the barn. Above them were cars on metal hangers that obviously moved by something mechanical if you wanted one. It saved on storage space. On the other side were computers and locked metal cases that probably held guns, ammunition and who knew what other kind of weapons to use against Grollics.

A female stood near a table tapping away onto a computer. She didn't even glance up when the door had opened or Michael had pulled in.

"Who's the hottie?" Rob asked.

"My sister," Michael barked.

"Sheesh. Can't a guy catch a break?" Rob stuffed his hat onto his head and opened the Jeep door, flipping the slide at the same time. The chair flipped forward so I could get out.

I scrambled out, clutching my bag with the wolf journal and stood close beside him. He slipped his arm over my shoulder. "Calm down, little Jamie, before you do something crazy."

Michael glared at the two of us before getting out of the car. He slammed his door shut and stomped over to Grace.

"I hear you, Michael. You don't have to shout." Grace still didn't look up as her fingers tapped away on the computer keyboard.

"What?" Rob's eyebrows rose as he glanced at them and then back to me.

"They can talk to each other in their heads. Like mental telepathy."

Grace spun around on her stool at the sound of my voice. "Rouge!" She raced toward me with her supernatural fast ability, only to skid to a stop when she noticed Rob. She sniffed and hesitated. "Who's he?"

"Rouge's brother." Michael grabbed a phone off the table and began flipping through its messages.

"What?" She stared at Rob, her head tilted to the side, her blue eyes bright. "Half-brother?"

"Full." Michael didn't even look up.

"Bentos' son?"

"Yes," I said, ready to protect her from him and vice versa.

Her eyes slowly moved up and down Rob. "Are you a Grollic?"

He smiled and winked at her. "At your service. I'm Rob, and you are?"

"Grace. I'm Michael's sister, and Rouge's best friend."

Did she just bat her eyelashes at him? I watched their interaction in disbelief. I swore they were flirting with each other!

"You're the other twin?" Rob stepped forward and held out his hand. "Hopefully the good half." He nodded toward Michael. "He's a miserable arse."

"And a lying sack of..." Grace caught herself just in time. She smiled. "Sorry." She reached out and rested her hand in his.

Rob surprised me by pressing her hand to his lips instead of shaking it.

"Don't you dare bite her!" Michael was instantly at Rob's side, a knife against his throat.

Rob's eyes burned to yellow, but he held himself where he stood. "I'm not going to."

"Michael!" Grace slapped her brother's shoulder with her free hand. "Let him be!"

"He's a Grollic!" Michael shouted.

"I can see that." She rolled her eyes. "He's also Rouge's brother. Cut him some slack."

"Yeah, cut me some slack." The corner of Rob's mouth pulled upward but he managed to hide the smile.

Michael moved away. His arm holding the knife came up fast as he drilled the weapon into one of the wooden beams across the barn. It sunk deep into the wood. "I'm going inside to shower." He turned and left the barn without another word and without giving me another glance.

Chapter 5

Grace watched him leave and then rushed over to me and wrapped her arms around me. "I'm glad you're okay. I wanted to come to Niagara Falls, but Caleb said I needed to stay back, and Michael didn't want me to come either." She glanced at Rob. "I think I know why now."

Rob's stomach growled. He gave her a sheepish smile. "Sorry."

She laughed and motioned toward the house. "Come on, let's get you some food. You must be famished! Michael wouldn't stop, right?" She shook her head. "He always does that."

"We ran into an unfriendly pack of wolves. Michael probably figured it was best to drive straight through till we got here."

I stared at Rob wondering why he was defending Michael. I thought he hated my boyfriend.

"I can throw together some bacon and eggs. Come on." Grace slipped her arm around both of us and pulled us toward the door beside the large barn door that had closed when I wasn't looking.

The inside of the house didn't have the same extra-ordinary appeal as the barn did. It literally was an old farm house, just very clean inside for somewhere that no one supposedly lived in. Old, antique furniture filled the front entrance and everywhere I seemed to look.

Michael was nowhere to be found.

Part of me wanted to go hunt through the house for him.

"Did you know Rouge was alive before she showed up at your door?" Grace asked Rob, completely distracting me from my train of thoughts. She led us to the large country style kitchen covered in ugly floral wallpaper.

"No. I mean, sort of. I knew I had a sister but didn't have any idea if she was alive or dead. My mother never told me what happened to her."

"You live with your mother?"

He gave her a slow single nod, obviously not quite sure how to respond.

"She died," I said, filling her in. "How much did Michael tell you? About what happened?"

"Not enough." She shot a dirty look toward the stairs where the sound of running water could be heard.

"Tell me about it," I mumbled.

Grace hugged me. "Sorry you didn't find your mom, or the answers you were hoping to find."

"I found Rob. He wasn't too keen on helping me at first..." I grinned and winked at him. "But he came 'round in the end."

"More like two rounds. One to Marcus' chest, the other to his head."

Grace spun around to give Rob an 'I'm-impressed' look. "You shot another Grollic?"

He shrugged. "I had to. He was going to kill Rouge."

"Very cool." She moved to the fridge. "I picked up some food. I thought you guys wouldn't be here until lunch." She made a face. "And I didn't know you were coming, Rob, or I'd have grabbed more. A steak sub okay?"

"I'll eat anything, I'm starving!" Rob accepted the sub she offered and sat down at the linoleum table. "What time is it, by the way?" he asked as he unwrapped the sub.

"Five thirty." I yawned and glanced toward the ceiling as the shower water above us turned off. Too early for a steak sub. I sat down at the table across from Rob and set my bag on the table. The Grollic book and my journal slipped out.

"What's that?" Grace asked.

"Wolf book, plus my lousy attempt at copying it."

"You still trying to translate it for Caleb?"

I ignored Rob's loud snort. He obviously disagreed with sharing anything with High Coven Leader Caleb. I didn't have the energy to argue that it was my journal, not a book for translating. I rubbed my eyes and rested my elbows on the table. "You guys mind if I jump in the shower? I need to wake up."

Grace patted my arm. "First room on the left is yours. I took clothes along for you. There's a suitcase opened on the bed. I haven't had time to put stuff in the closet."

"That's okay." I stood, the chair scraping against the floor as it slid. "I don't think we'll be staying here very long."

"You're probably right." Grace frowned at the stomping coming from above them. "What's he so angr—uptight about? I haven't seen him like this since the day Damon kidnapped you."

"Who's Damon?" Rob wiped his mouth with the back of his hand.

Grace flicked her wrist as if to dismiss Damon's importance. "A stupid, young, dumb Grollic who got what was coming to him. Did I mention he was an idiot?"

"Really?" Rob grinned, clearing enjoying her disgust.

"He was part of a pack on the west coast that clearly had no brains. He kidnapped Rouge. He didn't know who she was or her... her special ability."

I wanted to shower and Grace could fill Rob in on most of the story. "I didn't know much about anything back then. The Grollic journal kinda found its way to me. I had no idea what it was. I don't have a birthmark just below my collarbone."

Grace's head twisted in my direction but she said nothing.

"You're not marked?" Rob's hand went to the spot every Grollic carried their mark.

"Not on my chest." I'd kept the mark on my shoulder blade a secret from Michael. It didn't seem right to tell Rob before Michael. "Damon kidnapped me on my birthday. It would make sense to say it was planned but he had no clue it was my birthday. He knew I was the Seventh Mark, he just didn't know I had the power already." Neither did I at the time. Above me, something crashed to the floor, followed by a slew of colorful words. "Grace can fill you in on the rest. I'm jumping in the shower." I turned and headed up the stairs as the two of them started talking quietly.

Holding my breath at the top of the old winding wooden staircase I tiptoed to the first room on the left. A large suitcase sat on the bed, half empty, the clothes inside a mixed mess.

A shirt suddenly flew from behind the bed in the air and into the suitcase. Another slew of clothing articles got tossed into the suitcase. Michael straightened from behind the other side of the bed. He blinked in surprise before a scowl covered his handsome features. "Dropped the suitcase."

I walked over and grabbed a pair of red panties hanging on the bed post and quickly stuffed them into my pocket. Grace obviously assumed Michael and I would be sharing the room.

"How long have you known I was the Seventh Mark?"

Michael hesitated, throwing the last pile of clothes off the floor into the suitcase. "I didn't."

I sighed. "Whatever." I moved to the bathroom to shower.

Michael reached for my hand as I passed him. "I didn't know."

I stood and waited as he wrestled to organize his thoughts.

"This isn't a quick talk, Rouge. It's complicated."

"It must be. You've been lying to me since the first day we met. I'm going to jump in the shower. Maybe when I get out you'll have had enough time to consolidate another lie, or excuse, to explain it away." I pulled my hand out of his and hurried to the bathroom, closing the door behind me, purposely flipping the lock to the door as loud as I could. Luckily it was an old wooden door and the brass joint clicked noisily shut.

I flipped the shower on and stripped down as I waited for the water to get hot. The house was old but the bathroom had been modernized. The antique claw tub still acted as the bath and shower, but a new shower head and shower curtain ring surrounded it. If we weren't on the run or our lives in such a mess at the moment, I would have taken the time to enjoy the shower.

Instead I hopped in, cleaned and scrubbed the dirt and tiredness away before quickly washing my hair with the expensive looking bottle of shampoo and conditioner on the shelf by the window.

As the water rinsed the shampoo away, I give up on not trying to think. Michael had known what I was all along. He had to have. It made perfect sense. Why hadn't I realized that earlier? We met in a graveyard for Pete's sake. Why would a handsome-looking guy like him be there?

He was a Hunter.

That was why.

The realization hit me like a blow to the stomach. I lost my breath and leaned forward in the shower as if I'd been hit.

He had been hunting that night.

Looking for Bentos' daughter.

Hunting the Seventh Mark.

Chapter 6

Then why didn't he kill me? It didn't make sense. I shut the water off and reached for the top towel resting on the pile just outside the foot of the antique tub. Wrapping it around me, I grabbed a smaller one to squeeze the water out of my hair.

I tried to remember what happened that night almost a year ago. I'd been jogging and my ear buds had somehow managed to wrap themselves around a small angel statue's head. I snorted. It was like I had unintentionally been trying to strangle her. How ironic Hunters were descendants of angels.

Why else would Michael have been there, except to be hunting me down?

I had no clothes to change into, except for the red panties stuffed in my pocket. I pulled them on and then stared at the angry reflection looking back at me in the mirror. I wanted answers. If this was all some sort of game Michael was playing, set up by Caleb, to use me as a pawn, I wanted out.

I jerked the door handle and then remembered I'd locked it. Flipping the deadbolt I stomped into the bedroom. It didn't have the proper affect I wanted it to have with bare feet.

Michael had closed the bedroom door and stood staring out the window at the rising sun working its way over the Appalachian Mountains. "How was your shower?" he asked quietly, not turning around.

"Fine." I grabbed a pair of pants from the suitcase now sitting on top of the antique desk. Turning my back to Michael I slipped on a bra and red shirt that was loose around the neck. It slipped over my right shoulder. I lifted my shoulder to move it up and then ignored it when the collar part slipped over my shoulder again. It was the style and I had no intention of taking it off for something different. I hopped onto the bed and sat cross legged in the middle of it. I noticed my bag with the Grollic journal and my diary sat on the end of the bed. I reached for it and pulled out my diary. I had a pen inside the bag as well. I wrote fast, writing down how Michael and I had met that first night and what had happened in the past day.

Ten minutes later I slammed the book shut and tossed the pen by my bag. It landed and rolled perfectly back into it.

"What were you writing?" Michael asked, still standing by the window. He had turned so he could still look outside but watch me at the same time.

"Stuff."

He rolled his eyes and huffed. "This is ridiculous."

"You bet your ass it is!"

His eyebrows mashed together. "Excuse me?"

"You're acting like I'm the one who's been lying to you. Like you're the victim here." I jumped off the bed.

Michael took a step toward me. "You consider yourself a victim?" He shook his head. "And do you think you're the only one who's been lied to? That this is all about you?" His eyes burned bright blue, the pupils small against the darkness in his face. "What about you, Rouge? You have *nothing* to share with me?"

I matched his anger with my own. It burned and tightened deep inside my stomach. While his voice stayed low and deadly, mine rose. "You mean this?" I pulled the shirt over my left shoulder and twisted around. The mirror on the other side of the room showed me his face as he looked at the birthmark on my shoulder, in that spot low on the shoulder blade that was next to impossible to touch. My left breast pressed against the front of my shirt, trying to escape the pressure. I didn't care. "I never knew it was anything. Even when Damon kidnapped me and said I was the Seventh Mark. He thought it was on the same spot as his marking. Did you know that? Did you know the seventh son of the Vargulf Monstrums would be marked on their back? Did you know it would change on my birthday from a regular birthmark to one that looked burnt? Is that how you found me, by looking for the marking?"

Michael's face turned from anger to frustration. His fingers reached out but did not touch my skin. "I didn't know you had a mark. You never told me. When I saw it, I figured you would tell me on your own time. I never figured you would hide it."

"I. Would. Hide. It?" I spun around and glared at him. "You want to know why I never brought it up? Why I was scared to tell you?" I jabbed him in the chest with my finger. His muscles tightened and I tried not to notice how good he smelled. "You're a Hunter!! A hunter who kills Grollics! I'm a Grollic. I'm the one you and your almighty Higher Coven want dead. We can't be together! I didn't want to admit it to you, or to myself. If I told you about it, then I would be destroying us! So, I'm sorry I didn't talk to you about it. Or to your precious Caleb." I threw my hands up in the air.

Michael reached out for me but I pushed his hands away. "You are not one of them. You have the ability to control them. You could eliminate all of them."

I shook my head and stepped back. "What? You want me to kill them? Kill my brother?"

"No!" He grabbed my hand and held it tight. "I didn't mean your brother."

"Just every other Grollic. So you can be the hero who won the war?"

"That's not what I mean—"

"And you knew I was the Seventh Mark, didn't you? That's why you found me in the graveyard when I'd moved here." I wrenched my hand out of his. "You were hunting me, weren't you?"

"I... I... No! I was looking for..." He shook his head and his eyes closed. "You weren't supposed to be a girl."

"Excuse me?" The silence in the room grew deafening. "I wasn't supposed to be a *girl*?" The words escaped my lips in a quiet, clear, jeer.

Michael ran his fingers through his hair. "It's complicated, Rouge."

"Really? I hadn't thought my life had turned complicated the day I met you and then your sister." The sarcasm dripped from my words. "Was this all a ruse? You, your sister, all of you? A trap to keep me close so I would kill the Grollics?"

"No!" He glanced toward the window and then back at me. "I had no idea who you were! I mean..." He sighed. "I honestly did not plan on meeting you that night. Then you showed up and I tried to stay away. When that Grollic saw you the first time and didn't kill you, I knew you were different. I just didn't know how." His eyes danced back and forth as they stared at mine. "I tried to stay away," he whispered as his arms reached for mine. "I didn't know I'd fall in love with you." He sighed. "I love you, Rouge. Not what you are, but who you are. I'd give everything up to be with you if I had to."

I pushed up on my toes and pressed my lips against his. He pulled me tightly into his arms. "I love you," he said in between kisses. "I love you."

What did he mean when he said he would give up everything to be with me? Was Caleb threatening to disown him? To remove him as his understudy? Caleb was the leader of the Higher Coven, the oldest Hunter, and one of the originals. Michael was his understudy, expected to take his position should anything happen to him. Caleb didn't fancy me, but after everything that had happened in the past year, I thought we had come to some kind of understanding. Maybe I had been wrong.

I buried my head against his neck and rested my cheek on his shoulder. I loved him, but I couldn't tear him away from his family, or ask him to choose. I had no right.

Michael stiffened. He shifted and positioned himself in front of me to block the window. "Someone's here."

Chapter 7

"What?" My heart rate tripled its rate at his words.

He held his arm protectively against my chest as he moved to stand beside the window and then pushed me on the bed. "Stay there."

"Who?" I cocked my head trying to hear anything that sounded out of the ordinary. I heard nothing. Not even Grace and Rob talking downstairs. Had I heard them earlier? I couldn't remember.

Michael motioned to be quiet.

I rolled onto my stomach, ready to run if he told me to. "Is it a car?" I whispered.

He shook his head as he slowly opened the window with one hand. It effortlessly and soundlessly slid without complaint. Ironic for an old house. Michael dropped his knees slightly and suddenly disappeared through the opening of the glass.

I swore I blinked and he was gone. I couldn't hear him move on the roof nor was there a sound of him hitting the ground. I hesitated only a second before scrambling off the bed and staying low to the floor, I made my way to the stairwell, checking everywhere as I raced down the staircase to the kitchen.

Rob and Grace were gone. "Oh crap," I muttered before moving back into the hallway for the stairs. With my body pressed against the wall I shuffled toward the living room and peered in.

Empty.

Across the hallway, just before the staircase was one more room. Probably a formal dining room. I tried to see if there were lights on or movement of any kind inside of it. From my angle it appeared vacant but I couldn't be sure from where I stood shimmied up against the wall beside the living room. The fantasy wooden staircase railing partially blocked my view.

Where were they?

My heart panicked and its rhythm shot through the roof. If the Grollics found us leaving Niagara Falls, they could easily have followed us down here. What if one of them had bit Grace or Michael? Or attacked them both and dragged Rob away from the house?

I took a tentative step towards the front door and jumped back when a clicking sound came from the latch. The door knob slowly turned. Someone was trying to get in!

I grabbed the nearest object, ready to fight till the death with it.

I glanced down. *A candlestick? Really?*

Like a freakin' game of clue. Miss Peacock, in the living room, with the candlestick! I shifted and slid my fingers to the top, taking position like a baseball player. I hoped it would be a Grollic, I'd tell the thing to turn itself into a rug for the living room floor.

A long, muscular male leg appeared, followed by a brawny chest stepping through the door, as if he wasn't frightened of anything.

I raced forward, arms swinging the silver candlestick.

"What the—!" The guy ducked and covered his head.

My wild swing missed so I swung around and took aim again. Ready to swing if he moved. The stairs creaked behind me, warning that someone else was approaching from behind. "Stop!" I hissed, hoping it was a Grollic and they'd wait on the stairs.

No luck. It wasn't a Grollic. Whoever it was, they were now racing incredibly fast down.

I swung around, ready to kill. "Michael?"

He paused on the bottom step, his hands in the air. "I thought you were still upstairs in the room."

"Who's..." I glanced over my shoulder to a pair of bright blue eyes and a familiar cocky smile.

Seth!

"Do you mind putting that hundred year old weapon down?" He grinned and held his arms out.

His dark hair had a new style. He looked a bit older, if that was possible for a Hunter – maybe it was the maturity behind his eyes. He'd lost Tatianna because of Grollics in Port Coquitlam... because of me. Despite that, he still had the mischievous, troublemaker look that women were drawn to.

I dropped the candlestick and hugged him. "Seth! What're you doing here?"

He held me tight and chuckled. "Apparently trying to get myself killed again. One blow from you might be as deadly as a Grollic bite."

I pulled back and playfully punched him in the chest. "Don't tempt me."

Michael's hand slipped into mine and he gently pulled me close to him. "Found the scoundrel sneaking up in the front yard."

"Still worried I'm going to take your girl?" Seth laughed and leaned comfortably against the door frame. "And I wasn't sneaking! I was walking, and whistling I might add, as I headed up the drive. In plain sight."

"You could've been a decoy. With a hundred Grollics hiding in the trees around us."

Seth shot him a disgusted look. "I'm way too handsome to be a Grollic."

He was way too handsome to be real. Magazines couldn't photoshop a picture to make it look as nice as Seth.

"Not the point, idiot." Michael rolled his eyes and headed toward the kitchen with me in tow. He bent down to pick up the candlestick and put it back where I'd taken it from.

"Where's Grace?" Seth asked as he followed us.

"In the kitchen," Michael said.

"I was just in there." I glanced up the staircase as we passed. I hadn't thought to look up there. "She's not there."

Michael frowned. "I didn't see her, or Rob, outside."

"Who's Rob?" Seth moved to the fridge and pulled a beer out of it.

I opened my mouth to tell him but Michael cut me off.

"A Grollic Rouge's controlling."

Seth's eyebrows shot up. "Like a pet? Impressive."

"I'm nobody's pet!" Rob's voice thundered from behind me. He appeared, hair wet and clean clothes. He'd apparently just showered.

"Where's Grace?" Michael said, his voice tight as he fought to control it.

Seth laughed and pulled another beer out of the fridge, tossing it to Rob.

Rob caught it and twisted the cap off. "Thanks! I'm Rob. Who're you?"

"Seth. How'd Rouge talk you into coming to help us if she's not controlling you?"

"I'm her brother."

Seth nodded like it didn't surprise him.

"Her older brother," Rob added and grinned as he took a swig of beer. "Grace'll be down in a moment. She's just in the shower."

Oh crap. I glanced at Rob, then Michael and then back at Rob. Was he seriously trying to get himself killed?

Beer sputtered out of Seth's mouth. "Did you just say her older brother?"

"Yeah," Rob smirked.

"Same mother?" Seth wiped his mouth with his hand and slid it over his jeans. He leaned against the open door of the fridge.

"You got it."

"And f-father?"

"The one and only." Rob finished his beer and set it on the table before sitting down. "You mind handing me another one?"

"You have got to be kidding me." He pulled three brown bottles out of the fridge and set them on the table.

"Bit early, isn't it?" I asked as I moved to the fridge to see what was inside it. Beer, coke, subway sandwiches. I grabbed one marked BLT and a coke. Might as well join the club. I needed to eat and wasn't about to ask if there was a Tim Hortons around the corner. That was highly unlikely in America.

Michael sighed and sat down at the head of the table, Seth sat down across from Rob. All three twisted open their beer and clinked the necks of the bottles. I sat down on the counter and put the sub in the microwave to warm it up a bit.

"So what's the plan?" Seth asked.

"Why are you here?" Michael asked at the same time.

Rob and my gazes met. His eyebrows went up as I shrugged. I had no idea what was going on or what was going to happen.

Seth nodded toward the entrance of the kitchen. "Your sister asked me to come. Told me not to tell my guy and to get myself down here as fast as I could."

"Where were you?" I asked as I unwrapped my sandwich.

"Up north. Fishing." Seth grinned and winked at me.

"Who's your guy?" Rob asked.

"Seth's an understudy as well." I bit into my sub, ignoring Michael's dirty look.

"Seriously? Two of you in one room?" Rob leaned back in his chair and clasped his hands behind his head. "My old self is killing me for not shifting and reaching across the table to destroy both of you. I'd be revered more than Bentos himself."

Seth stiffened. The others wouldn't have noticed but from where I sat, I could see his back straighten slightly, like he was ready to pounce. "You can try it, little man. I doubt you'll have anything to bring back to your pack."

Rob raised his hands in mock surrender. "You don't have to worry. I no longer have a pack. Or," he said and smiled at me. "I've got a pack leader that's tougher than all the rest. I'll stick with her."

"Are you seriously Rouge's brother?"

"He is," I answered. "I also have the ability to control him. Speaking of which, are you able to turn again now, Rob? I tried setting you free back when the Grollics were attacking and didn't get a chance to ask."

"I'm all good. Thank you very much, lil' sis." His face turned serious. "Her real name is Jamie."

"It's Rouge." Michael was not in the mood to argue.

"Who gives a shit right now?" Seth shook his head. "Just tell me what the hell is going on and what we need to do. Caleb's going to go nuts when he finds out you have Bentos' son and we're keeping him safe... and alive." He reached for his beer. "Bentos is going to do worse when he finds out we have him too. It's all about to hit the fan."

"Caleb can't know we have him." Michael kept his face tight and unreadable.

"He's going to kill you." Seth frowned. "I'm not sure this is a good idea."

"Neither am I." Michael turned to Rob. "You killed Marcus. What's going to happen to your pack? You were their Alpha."

"They'll fight for a new Alpha and hunt me down. No wolf kills his own and lives to tell about it. Bentos is going to hear about it. He's going to know why. There's only one reason a Grollic would kill his own. Over a woman."

"I hear ya there, mate." Seth raised his bottle.

"Not quite, and I'm not your mate. I'm your enemy." Rob's eyes burned yellow as he clutched his beer tightly in his hand. "Bentos is going to know why I did it. He's going to come for me, and Jamie."

"Rouge," Michael corrected.

Chapter 8

"Jamie, huh? I like it. It fits you." Seth wagged his eyebrows as Michael shot him a stern look.

I ignored the bantering between them all and pulled my sub from the microwave, blowing on it in hopes of not blistering my tongue. Bentos being after me was something I was more than aware of, but the need to panic didn't feel ever-present. Somehow, somewhere deep inside of me I wanted the confrontation. Maybe I was going crazy.

"We need a plan and quickly." Michael took a long sip of his beer, his eyes moving over toward me as I yelped.

"Hot. I knew I was going to burn my tongue."

"You're impatient." Michael shrugged as I glared at him.

"As are you." Grace smiled and walked toward me, leaning against the counter and turning her attention back to the boys at the table. She clapped her hands and rubbed them together. "Bentos is coming, so what's the plan?"

"Well, I don't know what it means, but if we're all supposed to be a team, I guess I'm going to have to tell you guys I know how we defeat him." Rob shrugged and set his beer down, turning a little and nodded to me as if asking for permission to continue. I had no clue what he knew or didn't and wanted the information.

"What do you mean?" I slid off the counter and walked to the table, motioning for Grace to join me. I took a seat next to Rob and tucked my legs under me, Michael's eyes moving along me as I shifted in my seat.

"My mother used to always tell me it would be the strength of three that would ultimately defeat the seventh son, the *Vargulf*

Monstrum." Rob sucked his bottom lip into his mouth and spread his hands on the table.

I swallowed, the sudden dryness in my throat almost painful. How did he know the term? Did all Grollics know it? It was what had given me away to Damon last year. Maybe his—our—mother knew more about Bentos than any of us. Maybe Rob did too. "What's the power of three, Rob? You mentioned it before in the Jeep driving down here." I coughed, trying to clear my throat. "What's the power of three?" I repeated slightly louder.

Rob shrugged. "I don't know." He nodded toward Michael. "You're old as shit. What is it?"

Michael scoffed and pushed away from the table, rolling his shoulders he turned his attention to me. "Do you know?" When I shook my head, he sighed. "I don't know either, but I can talk to Caleb about it."

I reached for his arm. "I'd rather you didn't. At least not right now. He's not exactly a fan and something tells me that if mine and Rob's mom thought to put it in Rob's head, then this power of three thing might be able to take out Bentos. I don't think she meant for the information to get back to the Hunters." I was pretty sure the power of three thing had everything to do with me. That I needed three powers or something in order to defeat the evil bastard referred to as my father. He was stronger, smarter, older, and a whole lot more experienced in everything than I was. Shoot, wasn't I pretty much just a pup compared to him?

"Why do you assume that?" Seth asked, speaking again for the first time in a while. He was usually so much more talkative and yet the room sat heavy with unspoken fear by all of us.

I shrugged, slowly putting pieces of the puzzle together within my head as we conversed over it. "Rob and I are Grollic, I'm assuming our mother was as well."

"No," Rob interrupted. "She wasn't Grollic. Just human. Normal."

"Oh." That put my theory in the dust. I waved my hand. "But you're her son, and you're a Grollic. She probably hid it to protect you... and maybe me." I sucked in a quick, shaky breath. "Grollics are natural born enemies of the Hunters. I highly doubt Rebekah would have foreseen all of us sitting around a table together working through how to kill my father."

"And mine," Rob spoke.

"And our murderer," Grace added.

Rob raised his eyebrows but didn't say anything.

Seth pushed his chair back and leaned forward, resting his elbows on the table. "Let's just say, for shits and giggles, that this power of three is something we can figure out." Seth spun his empty bottle before him, his concentration on it as his voice droned on softly. "And we defeat Bentos somehow. Then what? Does all of his power go into you, Rouge?"

I went and grabbed my sandwich, needing something to do with my hands. The thought had crossed my mind a few times, but I pushed it away quickly due to the fear it caused. I really didn't know. I was having trouble controlling the small amount of power I had. I had no idea how to use it. If I were all of a sudden flooded with the vast amount of power my father held inside of him...

I looked up, scared that everyone would be staring at me. My gaze ignored the others and went straight to Michael as his brow bunched up. He was worried about the same thing.

"We don't know the answer to that." Michael moved to stand behind me, his hand rubbing my shoulder.

I leaned into it and finally looked around the table. "You're right. We don't. Not yet."

"Then we need to be prepared not just for this first step, but the next one too." Seth turned his attention to me and shot me his award winning sexy smile. "Whatever that means, we'll do it together. I've got your back. No matter what the Hunters say."

I smiled. He said that now, but he was an understudy like Michael. That opinion might change when Caleb and the others of the Higher Coven decided I wasn't going to help them much. I pushed the thought aside. We needed to concentrate on right now. Just staying alive seemed to be the main focus at the moment. "I think defeating Bentos is going to be way more difficult than pulling together the three whatevers we need. What if we don't know how to use the objects? Where is the training guide on all of this?"

"Could it be in the journal?" Michael asked.

"I never saw it in there." I think I'd have remembered what the power of three was. "The journal's about defeating, controlling and killing Grollics." I didn't want to make it sound impossible to defeat Bentos, but he had the power of controlling all Grollics, including Rob. What if he could control me as well? The thought scared the hell out of me.

"What would happen if he pulled Rob into the fight and he had no choice but to become an enemy?" Seth asked.

No one said anything.

I glanced at Rob and shuddered, hating the thought of finally finding someone that might be a pure part of my future only to lose him again. We would have to kill him if he stood in opposition to us on the battlefield, but could I do that?

I wasn't sure of anything, least of all that.

"Rouge, can I talk to you in private for a minute?" Michael leaned over my chair, his hand squeezing tightly on my shoulder.

"Yeah, sure." I stood and pointed to my sub. "Don't touch that or I will harm you all. Got it?"

"Someone throw the sandwich to me. I'm in the mood for something unpleasant today." Seth laughed at himself.

"I might be able to control the Hunters too." I gave him a stern look over my shoulder. At least it shut him up as he glanced at Grace for confirmation. Grace just shrugged and then winked at me as I passed her.

I walked close to Michael, almost bumping into him as he stopped at the top of the stairs, looking over his shoulder as if to check if I was behind him.

"You okay?" I asked, sliding my hands along his waist and pressing a kiss to his back.

He trapped my arms around his front with his own, a simple 'mhm' was all I got. He pulled from me and we walked up the stairs into the bedroom. I walked to the bed and sat down, tucking my feet under me again as he turned and pressed his back to the closed door.

My stomach growled loudly, the sound embarrassing like two cats fighting in a back alley. "Sorry. I should've brought the sandwich with me."

He smiled, his mind obviously on other matters. He reached up and ran his fingers through his hair. "I think we need to figure out this power of three thing, Rouge. I remember hearing something about it years and years ago, but can't pull the exact reference for some reason. Caleb will know what it is. I think it's important that we use all of our resources in this battle. I don't think we have a choice."

"No!" Somehow having Caleb here would be dangerous. "You involve Caleb and he's going to use Rob as bait, if he doesn't kill him first. I am not risking that." I sighed. This is what he wanted to talk to me privately about? "We just heard about this power of three thing. Give me a couple days to see if I can find out more about it and then if nothing else, we can maybe think about calling Caleb to ask for information."

"Where are you going to look for information on it? Rob doesn't seem to know anything more than the reference and you're not going to go looking for your father, who I'm sure is aware of this idea that there is something out there great enough to defeat him."

"He wouldn't share information on that anyway." I laughed at his silliness. "Maybe there's more information in this wolf journal than I'm giving it credit for."

I reached over and picked it up, laying back on the bed and holding it above my face as I opened the pages. A soft whisper of power seemed to fill the room.

Michael walked toward me, stopping at the edge of the bed and tapping his fingers on my knees. I looked up at him, his expression sorrowful.

"What?" I moved to my elbows, setting the book down and concentrating on him. He was a beautiful disaster, so much angst and worry pent up in the strong body of this handsome man.

"I'm just still chewing on your earlier explosion." He slid his hands up my thighs, his fingers stopping midway as his eyes burned brighter.

"What part of it is bothering you so much?" I reached up and pulled him toward me.

He moved onto the bed, hovering just above me as he watched me for a few moments before speaking. "The part where you've convinced yourself we can't be together."

I pulled him down and he reclined, his body pressed firmly to the top of mine. I opened my legs to make room for him and leaned up, brushing my lips across his as sadness tugged at my heart. "And you think we can be?"

"I know I don't see a future where you're not a part of it. Simple really."

"Is it?" I sighed softly, enjoying him being so close. He was magnificent, the structure of his features leaving no doubt that his inheritance was heavenly.

"I think it can be. If we just decide to stop letting that be a conversation we resort to. Nothing in my mind can pull us apart. I know we have a lot left to do, and I know you're scared about the power that is most likely coming your way, but I'll be with you to figure it out. If you let me."

"I'd pretty much let you do anything," I teased. "But it's not just me and you, Michael." I sighed, the sound falling flat as my heart constricted. "It's Caleb and Sarah. It's Grace and Rob and Seth. There are innocent Grollics out there under Bentos' control. There are so many people involved. If it were us we could just run forever, but everyone is involved. Caleb has placated us to believing he would be okay with our union, but you know it's not true. It spits in the face of all he stands for. It's only a matter of time and we're going to be forced to make a stand for who we are, which is going to leave us turning our back on each other or the other parts of our lives, including all those other people." I inhaled and let the air out in a loud huff. I didn't want to have this conversation. Not before, not now, not in the future. And here we were, lying on a bed talking about it.

"When did you get so wise?" He twirled one of my curls around his finger over and over.

I smiled and pulled him down, pressing softly against his chest just as his eyes closed. "I love you. Let's just have what we can for today, and then work to defeat Bentos before he comes for everyone we love."

Michael opened his eyes, the electric blue almost shocking me silent. It did every time. "You want to go after him instead of sitting here and waiting?"

"Yes, when the time's right. Let's figure this power of three thing out, gather the three things we need that contain this immense power and train how to use them. Maybe the Grollic journal is one of the three things. We're already a third of the way there." It made sense. "We'll leave here if we have to, but once we're somewhat confident that we can do this... no more running. We stop and fight."

"I don't run. At least, I never considered myself a coward, or a runner. Then I met you and now all I want to do is hide you somewhere safe. How did you manage to change me into this... this quivering lump of mush?" His smile was radiant as he slid his hands into the back of my hair, his fingertips pressing softly as he lifted my face to his.

"Admit it," I teased. "You've always been this way." I knew it was far from the truth. He was the strongest person I had ever met.

"So beautiful," he whispered and leaned down, his lips soft on mine. He pressed his tongue to my bottom lip, nudging me to open my mouth and let him in.

I did and felt the air slip from the room as he deepened the kiss, the soft groan leaving him almost undoing me. Chill bumps raced down my skin as my fingers dug into his back, his actions sensual and awakening parts of me that left me scared. I pulled back after a few more moments, my heart almost beating out of my chest. "We need to get back downstairs," I whispered, breathless.

"Do we?" He leaned down and brushed his nose from the base of my neck to my ear. "Thank you for coming clean on the marking on your back. I've been waiting for you to trust me a little more."

I shifted, forcing him to look at me. "I want to trust you completely."

"I want that too."

"Then come clean with what you know and I will." I reached up, touching the side of his face and wishing like hell that the future really did feel like it would keep us together. Something inside of me screamed the opposite, but I swallowed the worry. Now wasn't the time. A happily ever after wasn't in line with what we were headed into, just not yet at least. This wasn't a fairytale. I wasn't Red Riding Hood.

Chapter 9

I headed down the stairs on shaky legs, my body still wishing for the firm press of Michael against my front and the soft bed to my back. Too many people sat downstairs to let our quick conversation turn into a heated make-out session, but one was way overdo. I glanced back up the stairs at him. He smiled down at me, though I could see the worry in his eyes.

I had let my last request for him to come clean on everything stay dormant between us. He hadn't responded, and I knew it was because he didn't want to start another argument. The fighting between all of us was wearing us down faster than running for our lives.

I walked into the kitchen and skidded to a stop. Michael ran into the back of me as my hands grinded into my hips. I glared around the table. "Where's my sub?"

"Don't know what you're talking about." Seth shrugged and looked away quickly. Too quickly.

"Yep. Me either." Rob stared at the table before him, tapping a rhythm on the wooden structure.

"They split it and ate it in two bites each. I couldn't get to them fast enough." Grace sat on the counter, a large clipboard in her hand.

"What?! I'm starving too, you know! Jerks!" I walked over and popped each of them in the back of the head as they burst into man-giggles. *Disturbing.*

My eyes shot toward Michael as I caught him chuckling, so I pinned him with a stare. He looked over at me as the smile dropped from his mouth and he nodded, turning to the guys. "That's unacceptable. Don't touch my girl's food again or I'll beat you senseless." The corners of his mouth curved upward. "Have you heard her stomach when she's hungry? Scarier than an Alpha Grollic in heat."

"Hey!" Rob called out. "That's unacceptable!"

The microwave sounded as Grace skidded over the counter to open it. "I made you another. Don't burn your tongue on this one."

"Thank you. At least *someone* here cares about me." I looked over my shoulder as the choruses of 'I do' started. I pointed to her lap. "What's with the clipboard?"

She leaned against the cupboards behind her and pulled a pen out from behind her ear, tapping the board for a minute as she stared at me. She was deep in thought and there was no way to effectively pull her out until she was ready for me to. I shrugged and pulled the hot sandwich out, sighing softly as the pain in my stomach increased. Now to wait for the freaking thing to cool... again.

"We need to move every day unfortunately." Grace held up her hand to stop the groans coming from the men.

"We don't run." Michael leaned against the counter, his playful mood all but gone.

"Well, I don't know what else to tell you." Grace frowned as she stared at the clipboard. "This is new for me too, brother."

Seth snapped his fingers. "What about the underground facility in Miami? We could race toward it, slip underground without Bentos knowing where we are. It's got lots of protection around it."

"That would be fine if Rouge wasn't a tracking beacon." Grace reached over and rubbed my arm. "Sorry, sister."

"How is she a tracking beacon?" Michael asked.

"It's only when you use your power that he can pinpoint you, Rouge." Rob leaned back on his chair, balancing on the rear two legs.

Michael reached out and touched the side of my neck.

I leaned into his touch. "Then we've got a problem. Every time I get angry I start using it without knowing I'm doing it. How do you learn to harness it, if the only one who can teach from experience is the one trying to hunt us down and kill me?" I grabbed my sub and moved toward the hallway. I needed some space.

"I don't know, but we'll find out," Grace called to me as I left the room.

"I'm just going outside on the porch to eat my sub. I'm NOT running away." I needed time to think, needed fresh air and to eat my sub before anyone else did. I lifted the plate with my sub on it to my nose and breathed in deeply as I pushed the front door open and slipped out into the mid-day calm. The weather was perfect, the sun not pushing through all of the massive trees that sat around the property, but providing coolness and shade.

Michael was right about us running. It wasn't as if we could spend the rest of our days trying not to be discovered. Bentos was beyond powerful. Our Jeep and all the gas in the world wasn't going to keep him at bay much longer. I looked over my shoulder as the door opened.

"You want company?" Michael stood in the open door.

He looked like he had lots on his mind. He and Grace probably needed to do some planning or locate all their secret hideouts throughout the country. "I'm okay. Get done what you need to do."

Relief crossed his face, but only for a moment before he covered it and made it unreadable again. "You want your book?"

"I'll get it if I do, but thanks." I tucked a strand of my hair behind my ear, his smile making me feel loved, which I didn't deserve, but was happy to have.

"I'm here if you need me. Just call, I'll be right beside."

"Ditto." I watched him go before setting the plate down on the small table on the porch and took my sandwich with me as I walked around to the side of the house and then continued down a small path that led from the house towards the backyard. The woods thick with trees offered shade and comfort. I knew better than to go off into the woods by myself, but I could just hang out along the edges.

I lifted the sandwich to my lips, being careful to take a tentative, small bite before blistering my tongue again.

A bird sang high above me in the trees and I tried to find it, wanting to accept the serenity of the moment, but not quite able to push back the sense of foreboding sitting heavy on me. I knew Bentos would come, so why did it feel like that wasn't the only sucker punch I was waiting to get hit with? What else could possibly come our way that would be worse?

I found an old wooden park bench a little further down along the backyard. It barely looked like it was holding up, so I gingerly sat down and scanned the area around me, looking for something that might jump out and try to attack. Peace seemed to be a relative lie lately. Never offering itself for more than a fleeting moment or two. I just wanted five minutes to sit and eat my sub. Just five minutes.

The sound of the door slamming just up the path caused me to growl. *Now what?*

"You out here?" The sound of Rob's voice floated over to me.

I found myself less annoyed than I thought I would be. "Yeah. I'm over here, you sandwich eating ass."

He laughed loudly, the sound warm and enjoyable. I kind of wished we could have had a chance to grow up together, it might have been fun. He jumped off the back porch of the house and jogged over. He plopped his butt down on the long ago emptied cement bird bath close to me. The structure shifted slightly and I automatically reached for him.

"Whoa... shit." He laughed and placed his hands on the circular rim, his eyes wide.

"I almost dropped my sub!" I laughed. "It could have fallen in the dirt."

"I'd still eat it."

"Of course you would. You're disgusting." I chuckled again. "I wouldn't and I'm starving. If you so much as look at this sandwich..." I pretended to give him the evil eye.

"You'll what?" He shook his head and chuckled. "I'm twice your size."

"I'll turn you into a frog." I started to remind him that I had the power to control him, but something wasn't right with me being able to do that. It would break down our relationship for sure if I continued to use it against him. I needed to learn how to control myself before I threatened to control others. How much damage could I do if I wasn't careful?

Take out a whole pack of Grollics with nothing more than a few words.

I shuddered at the remembrance of the situation in Port Q, the event scarring me far more than I let on. "It's not fair," I muttered softly to myself.

"I'm not really going to eat your sandwich. Don't be dumb." Rob laughed as I turned to him. I must have missed some of the conversation by his response.

"Oh, I know you're not." I lifted the sub and took a large bite out of it.

"What did Michael tell you when he pulled you aside before?" Rob glanced back to see if anyone was around. Satisfied, he continued, "Did Michael give you anything on the power of three when you guys disappeared?"

"No." I took another bite and chewed for a moment, holding my finger up to get Rob to wait for a minute for my reply. I swallowed and wiped at my mouth, the food feeling as if it slammed into the empty hole in the middle of my body. "He didn't know. He wanted to call Caleb." I don't know why Michael wanted the moment alone with me, except maybe to just be together without anyone. It kinda seemed strange now.

"Caleb is never going to truly help you, or me. He's the king of our enemies, just as much as Bentos is. Caleb wants more than anything to put us out of commission. It's his whole purpose. That Michael would expect him to act differently just because he cares for you and Caleb cares for him seems very naive to me. It's stupid."

"I asked him not to talk to Caleb until we know more." I swallowed my need to defend Michael and picked up the sub, diverting my attention from my brother for a minute until my temper cooled back down.

"Where are we going next?"

"I don't know. Michael doesn't want to run, he hates it. But until we know what we're doing, I guess we have to keep moving. Once we figure out how to stop Bentos, then we can fight."

"I'm ready for that." Rob rolled his shoulders, his dark hair picking up as the wind blew.

I stuffed my hand deep into my pocket. It wanted to reach over and ruffle his hair like he was a little kid. "Do you always keep your hair long?"

"No, but I've been a little preoccupied. There was shit going on before you showed up. I had to take care of my pack..." His voice trailed off as he realized he was no longer an Alpha. He sighed. "The haircut is on the list, but not near the top." He rolled his eyes and swatted a fly away. "You know, you look a lot like Rebekah."

His words caught me off guard, the information less comforting than I cared to express. "Oh yeah?" I looked like my mother? Somehow I figured I looked like Bentos.

"Yes. She had copper curls too and a nice smile, when she managed to allow a little happiness into her life." He glanced over at me before looking up at the sky. "She was kind and fierce, loving and everything someone could want in a mom."

"She was?"

"Not really. She seemed lost most of the time but she did love you and me fiercely. Life just terrified her. Bentos terrified her. You being alive terrified her. She needed to find courage, just never got the chance."

Emotions I didn't want swarmed through my stomach. "I wouldn't know. I never met her."

"She gave you up because she had to, Jamie. She didn't abandon you. You have it all wrong." He jumped off the bird bath and came and sat beside me. Surprisingly the bench held both our weight.

I couldn't let go of how I'd felt so alone all my life. Michael and Grace had changed that and filled the void, but all those years of believing a lie, was I just supposed to accept this change? A mother who cared so much for my safety that instead of running with me and protecting me herself, she tucked me in the world of half-hearted humans and hoped for the best? The foster system sucked. I hated every minute of it. "Whatever. Felt like abandonment to me." I licked at my lips and changed the subject. "You seriously don't know anything about this power of three thing?"

"No. I wish I did. Rebekah used to say: 'To defeat the greatest evil you need to gather the power of three and stand when the time comes'. She made me memorize the damn thing when I was like seven."

"Gather?" I finished the last of my lunch and stretched out my legs as the sun broke through a tiny crack in the cover above us. "Then it's something physical we need to find."

Rob nodded, his face thoughtful. "You can't gather inanimate objects really, right?"

"That would make sense." I ran the saying through my head again. "What about the part where she told you to stand? Only people stand, right?"

"A lamp stands..." He laughed and I swatted at him. He caught my hand and pretended he was going to bite it. One eye turned yellow and the other stayed amber.

I laughed. "How'd you do that?"

He shrugged. "I don't know. Used to practice in the mirror. It's kind of like winking."

"It's freaky."

Rob gave me a smug look. "I got all kinds of talents. Sixth sense... sixth son... same thing you know."

"Whatever." I pushed my shoulder against his.

"Rouge?"

The tone of his voice had changed. "Yeah?"

"I know we have a tough road ahead of us and we don't know each other, but I'm here to protect you with my life. Pack is— pack was pack, but you're my blood, my mother's blood and I'll not let anything happen to you."

My eyes filled, his words rushing to try and tear down my walls. To not be alone in the world and questioning everyone would be bliss. It should be Michael I felt that with, but he was hiding something, he was always hiding something. Maybe my brother was the connection I needed, the path to healing my heart I so desired.

"Am I breaking something up?" Michael's voice was sarcastic, his eyes narrowed a little too much for my liking. He stood, arms crossed, glaring down at the two of us across the lawn.

How much had he heard?

"Aren't you always?" Rob scoffed and laid back against the bench, winking at me before closing his eyes. He turned his face toward the sky as if he enjoyed the scorching glare of angels far more than the heat of the sun above them.

Chapter 10

Michael tossed something at me, the object flying fast as I sat up to catch it. The journal. I nodded, grasping his hint. We didn't have time to lay around and try to find our courage. If we wanted this battle to take place and the running to stop, we needed to find a solution to stop Bentos.

With the power of three being the only thing we knew that might help, it was time to see if the wolf journal had anything to help. Too bad I couldn't read all of it.

"See what you can find. We'll stay here tonight, but we leave in the morning." Michael pinned me with his stare, his dislike of Rob sitting all over his handsome features.

"Leaving already? I kinda like this place. It's so... country." The sound of Rob breathing in deeply caused my lip to turn up.

"You're more than welcome to stay behind and guard the house. Fine by me." Michael shrugged and turned.

Rob mimicking him in a rather high-pitched voice didn't sound like Michael at all. "Stay behind n' guard the house."

"Watch it!" Michael yelled over his shoulder.

"I'm a Grollic. Not a dog," Rob muttered.

I couldn't help but watch Michael walk away, the strong muscles of his back pressing against his t-shirt, his blond hair almost seeming to shimmer every time the sun hit it. What he saw in me was beyond understanding, but I'd take it as long as he let me.

"Not to your own ears, but Jamie and I heard something pretty much like my rendition of you."

Mortified, I didn't know where to look or what to say.

"It's Rouge." Michael's voice grew soft as he left.

I watched him leave, torn between going to talk to him and staying here with Rob. I wished the two of them could get along. I elbowed Rob. "Don't mock him anymore. It's not cool."

"Fine. I'll try not to." Rob rolled his eyes before letting them focus on the book in my hand. "How'd you end up with the journal again?" He sat up, reaching over to touch it.

I jerked it away out of habit, a look of surprise running across his features.

"Sorry." I extended it, my heart beat racing at the idea of him touching it. Why did it feel so intimate, like something I should hide away and treasure only for myself? That thought alone should have me handing the damn thing over to Michael for safe keeping, but did I trust him with it?

No one but you...

Rob shrugged and clasped his hands together, raising them high into the air and seeming to ignore my offering to touch the book.

"You ignoring me?" He smirked and dropped his arms.

"Yeah." I opened it to a random page, scanning the foreign language, the images blurring a little as I concentrated on the curve of the first letter. I blinked a few times and looked up, a slight pressure in my head. Surely I could push past the blockage that held me back from understanding what it said. If my father had gifted me, even grudgingly and not by his choice, all of this power because I had the Seventh Mark, then everything I needed to decipher the words lay inside of me. How to unlock them had become the question. I'd unlocked bits and pieces before, why couldn't I now?

"Jamie?"

"Call me Rouge please. Jamie's not my name." I glanced over at him, Rob jolting back a little from me.

"What the hell?" He moved from the bench.

"What?" I dropped the journal in my lap and swatted at my hair and face. "Is it a spider? I hate bugs."

He reached for me, stilling my arms. "No. Your eyes turned oily black, like the cover of the journal. What did you do?"

I shook my head slightly, blinking like crazy. "Is it gone?"

He nodded, his mouth hanging open. "What'd you do?"

Feeling like nothing had happened, I wasn't sure if he was teasing me or really scared. "I tried to focus on the words. I can only read certain parts. It's driving me insane." I growled in frustration and picked the book back up. My eye color was the least of my concerns.

"Do the words make sense when you first look at them or do they shift into focus?"

"Lately none of it makes sense, but that's because I'm fighting who I am." How did I know that?

"Then stop fighting." He smiled as I looked up at him.

"I don't know how."

"Accept it. Own it. Use it." He moved beside me, leaning over as I opened the book again.

"Nothing but jumbled symbols and signs here, and here, and here." I flipped through, Rob's finger stopping me as he touched the top of one of the pages. He jumped back and hissed, lifting his finger to his mouth and blowing on it. "What the hell was that?"

I held my place in the book and moved off of the bench. "What's happened?"

"Why didn't you tell me it would?"

"Would what?"

"Burn me!" He stuck his finger in his mouth, pulled it out quick and began blowing on it.

"I didn't know it would do that. Actually, I think you're the first Grollic I've seen touch it." I brought it toward him again and he jumped away from it. "Hey, I'm still figuring all of this out." I sighed. "Is the skin melted from your finger?"

"It's probably half gone. I swear I can feel bone." He glanced down at his finger, turning his hand over. "It's... It's not."

"Then stop crying like a baby." I smiled and glanced at him, unable to help myself from chuckling at his pain. He growled a warning, but I ignored him, walking a few steps away as my eyes moved across the triangle at the top of the entry on the page I'd bookmarked with my finger. "This the triangle you were pointing at before the book laid a hurting on you?" I looked over my shoulder and got the bird flipped at me. "Classy."

"Yes. It's gotta be the power of three. Three corners... points... whatever you call them."

I began to pace, an idea forming in my head. "Say three people were fighting together against a group of attackers. What's the best military position to take?"

"That's easy, you go for higher ground."

"Say you can't do that. Say you're surrounded. You need eyes on all of the enemy right?" I wasn't a military person, but the idea in my head seemed to think I knew something about it. "If there were three people fighting together they would put their backs toward one another."

Rob nodded. "Then you would have eyes and ears on everyone if you worked together."

I snapped my fingers. "Exactly! Three people facing three directions. It would create a triangle!" I made the shape with my hand.

"Except you could only fight that way for so long. If you're surrounded by a pack of Grollics, and Bentos is one of them, you're pretty much screwed."

I rubbed my thumb along the image, the black ink fading to red and back to black. A soft gasp left me, my eyes widening as I tried it again.

Nothing.

"Try to focus and read something from that page, Jamie."

"Rouge."

"Whatever."

I looked up and glared at him. He held his hands up and took a few steps toward me. It was my turn to growl.

He grinned and nodded. "Nice. Very Grollic-like. You'll need to learn to foam at the mouth, too." He chuckled.

I ignored him as the diary began warming in my hands. I looked back down. "You've not seen me early in the morning," I jested, my thought long removed from the silly conversation with my brother. Something inside of me whispered the truth of this page, of this entry. The power of three... the triangle. It had to be perfectly balanced to stand strong. None of the sides would be able to bend or break, or be less effective than the others.

I squinted, calling into the depths of my mind to bring the words to life. Nothing.

"What're you doing?" Rob asked, his voice seemingly distant.

"Show me what I want to see," I whispered. The wind blew around me, the world fading slightly as the words just below the symbolic picture turned crimson and lifted off the page. I yelped and dropped the book, the world around me went dark. I froze. What the heck had just happened? I tried blinking but everything stayed black. "Rob?"

"I'm right here. Just breathe. Your eyes are black again. Can you see anything?" His hand touched my wrist lightly.

I blinked frantically, my heart racing as fear washed over me in suffocating waves.

I see you...

The world came into view and I looked around, searching for who might be watching us.

"Rouge, what did it say? Could you read any of it?"

I stopped turning and stared at Rob, the air so hard to breathe. "I only got the title of the entry. You're right. It said 'Power of Three'."

He waved his hand, annoyed I wasn't telling him everything. You didn't need to be a rocket scientist to figure out that something had just transpired. "What else happened?"

I didn't know exactly, nor was I ready to talk about it. Could Bentos pinpoint me when I read the book? Or was it the power I had to pull forth from deep inside myself to have it make any sense? "I don't know." I was terrified. "I think I need to lay down. I feel sick to my stomach." I clutched my stomach trying to fight the bile rising in my throat at the same time.

Rob picked up the book and tossed it to me, yelping again as he burned himself. I caught it and moved toward the house, the forest seeming darker and more ominous all of a sudden. I didn't want to tell Rob about the strange voice. Should I tell Michael?

I knew one of two things; either the book was talking to me, or Bentos was.

Rob opened the door and tried to tease me. "You feel sick because you ate a twelve-inch sub. Piggie."

He was being stupid, but I appreciated the distraction. I popped him in the chest and moved toward the stairs.

Michael appeared at the opening to the kitchen and he looked past me to Rob.

"We need to change a tire on the Jeep. You any good with those types of things?"

"I lived in the poorest part of town but everyone I knew there drove a nice car." He straightened and saluted Michael. "I can change all your tires and wash your windows in twenty minutes flat."

I turned and rolled my eyes at Rob before making my way up the stairs.

"Good, just the one tire then." Michael's voice followed me, the sound of his feet moving up the stairs behind me giving comfort.

"I'm going to lay down." I walked into the bedroom. "I feel kind of sick. Maybe it was the sub," I lied.

"Mind if I come with you?"

"Not at all, but I'm serious about trying to take a nap."

"I understand." He moved in behind me and closed the door as I crawled up on the bed and snuggled up on what I figured was my side. He moved in and curled up around my back, his arm wrapping around me and pulling me in close. He moved the hair from my neck and pressed a few soft kisses on my skin as my eyes began to flutter.

"I'm scared," I whispered, my voice not sounding at all like my own.

"I know. But Rouge, I'm here with you. I'm not going anywhere. Neither is Grace, and we couldn't get rid of your mangy brother if we tried."

I chuckled, the warmth of Michael's embrace pulling me deeper into the need for rest. I needed to come clean with him about everything that was happening inside of me, but what if it scared him? What if he rejected me simply because he wouldn't know any better than I did how to deal with all of it?

"Did you find anything in the journal, Rouge?" He didn't sound convinced I would. He kissed just below my ear and I turned in his hold, tucking myself against the front of his body as we lay on our sides. He pulled me in closer and entwined his legs with mine. I wished I weren't in jeans so I could feel more of his skin, the soft warmth of him always leaving my world spinning out of control.

"I found the page that talks about the power of three."

He jerked back, looking down at me as I glanced up at him. My eyes started to shut again, my body feeling as if it weighed a thousand pounds.

"What did it say? What are the three objects that we need?"

"I don't know. I dropped the book when it came to life."

"It came to life? Explain." He pulled farther from me and I grumbled, reaching up and pulling him back.

"I'm tired. I'll talk about it later." I tucked my face against his t-shirt again and breathed in deeply, wanting him to be my reality and nothing else. "I can't talk about it now. Please." I pressed closer to him. "I'm scared... terrified."

For once he didn't argue. He simply held me and kissed the side of my head as darkness invaded my thoughts and sleep pulled me down to lay hold of my fear.

Chapter 11

When I woke Michael was gone, the room having grown colder. I sat up, the darkness around me nothing to fear and yet I couldn't convince my beating heart of that. I bolted out of the bed and ran to the door, opening it fast and slipping out into the lit hallway. I pressed my back to the door and closed my eyes, taking long, greedy breaths. Someone approached from my left.

Turning, I raised my hands to prepare for a fight I was sure to come.

"What is up with you trying to kick my ass today?" Seth laughed and moved toward me, pushing my fists down before pulling me into a hug. He brushed my hair back as concern filled his handsome face, his eye color lighting up slightly. "You're hot."

"Don't let Michael hear you say that." I sighed, trying to rein in my fears, which felt completely out of control.

"No... I mean, you are hot, but your skin's burning to the touch. You getting a fever?"

"Just sweating in my sleep thanks to my horrid dreams." I reached up and touched my face, pulling from him and shrugging. At least the warmth hid my embarrassment for assuming he was hitting on me. "Feels normal to me."

"You need something for that fever. Everyone is pulling dinner together. Come down with me?"

"Let me go splash water on my face and I'll be right there." I turned and headed back into my room to use the restroom. My legs felt sore, like I had run a couple of miles in the snow – backwards. *What's wrong with me?*

The bright light of the restroom stung my eyes as I pulled the door closed. I turned and glanced at myself in the mirror as I turned the cold water tap on the faucet. "Yep... still me."

I leaned forward and widened my eyes. Hazel mixed with amber stared back at me, nothing out of the ordinary. *Nothing unusual.* I leaned in further as I noticed the ache in my throat, almost as if something was pushing its way out of me. I gripped the side of the sink and whimpered as a string of words left my lips, my eye color slowly fading to black. Nothing around me held color or substance, but I could still see myself.

It was the world behind me that scared me silent.

A war was coming. It was just me and my friends against Bentos. It was the Hunters and the Grollics. Hot climate, no reprieve from the heat. *Florida.*

I released the sink and turned toward the battlefield in my mind, the image fading fast. A loud knock at the door caused me to scream, the door opening and Michael plowing in before I could right myself. I shut my eyes tight so he wouldn't see.

"What the hell's going on?" He reached for me, pulling me to him and pressing his lips to my hair. "What's happening? You were screaming like someone was murdering you."

I took a long breath. I needed to get it together or no one would believe me when the time came and I needed them to.

When would this war happen? I'd had a premonition of some kind. Whatever I saw, it was going to happen.

"Rouge, talk to me." Michael shook me. "What's happening?" He pressed the back of his fingers to my head as he moved into the small bathroom. "You're burning up."

"Just tired I think." I turned and opened one eye to peer into the mirror. It was its normal amber-hazel color. I let the other open up as well. Thankfully Michael didn't notice.

"So tired that you're screaming up here by yourself?"

"Nightmare." I pulled from him and turned the still running water off. "Where's Rob?"

"He and Grace are working in the barn, fixing up a vehicle for us."

"Did he change the Jeep tire?"

"Still working on it, I believe."

"I thought he needed twenty minutes."

Michael smirked. "He did too." His face turned serious again. "Don't skirt the subject. Are you seriously okay?"

"I'm fine. Let's go downstairs. I'll need a glass of water or something." I moved out of the bathroom, Michael staying close to my side and reaching for my hand as we descended the stairs. He didn't say anything, but the worry on his face was apparent.

"Everything all right?" Seth walked from the kitchen as he wiped his hands on a white cloth.

"Yeah, just having nightmares."

"While you're awake?" Michael asked, tilting his head to the side. He released my hand and pulled a chair out for me to sit on. "Start telling me what's going on." He wanted in and it was overdue time to let him know.

I sighed, exhausted in a strange way. I sat down. "I guess they're more like visions." I watched Michael sit down across from me.

"Did something change to cause that?" Seth flipped a chair around and sat on it so he could lean his arms over the backing.

The smell of tomato sauce and garlic filled my senses and my stomach growled loudly.

"Seth, go get the others for dinner," Michael spoke, leaning back and pulling bread from the oven. His eyes never left my face.

Seth stood and headed out of the kitchen.

"Start talking." Michael crossed his arms over his chest.

I glanced over at the large pot of spaghetti, my hunger almost overwhelming me all of a sudden. I breathed in deeply and turned to look up into the most handsome face I'd ever seen. He was all I had, and the only one who loved me for who I was. "I don't know what's happening. Earlier, when I was outside with

Rob, something weird happened when I was looking at the book. Rob said my eyes turned completely black. I don't know. I'm not sure I even believed him. Then, just upstairs, I had this vision-thing."

Michael nodded. Thank goodness he didn't look at me like I was going crazy. "What about the journal? Did it do this to you?"

"Sometimes I think that damn thing is coming to life! I don't mean literally. It just..." I sighed, not sure how to explain it to Michael. "It's always felt like it belongs to me. Like it's a part of me. You know how a kid carries a blanket around forever, even though it's tattered and torn and gross to others, the kid thinks it's golden? That's how I feel about the journal."

"I don't know what you mean by coming to life."

"It's warm, always warm and comforting to me. But it burned Rob when he touched it. I don't know if it's because he's a Grollic or the sixth son or what. You've never hurt yourself on it. Neither has Caleb."

"Maybe it's just meant for your eyes only."

Speaking of eyes... "It made my eyes change color. To black." I rushed, not letting Michael interrupt me. "And it speaks, which scares the heck out of me."

"Wait up... it burns other people? And speaks?" He moved back, pressing his fingers to his forehead. "I need details and Rouge, we need to involve Caleb. This stuff is out of my league. He would know how to read the book or how to train you to read it."

"No! He won't! He doesn't know how, you know that. Remember I gave him the book to look at before. He probably brought it to his office, had some experts try to read it and burned a bunch of Grollics to see if they could read it." I shook my head. "That's why he's kept me around. To figure out the book and to kill the Grollics. I'm the tool to fix everything for him."

"We'll talk about this later." Michael jumped up. "Not in front of the others."

Noise came from the front before he finished speaking. Everyone piled in the kitchen. Rob looked like he had been dipped in mud and grease. The smile on his face quickly told me that he and Grace were getting along, perhaps better than Michael might approve. She took a seat next to me, looking perfect as per usual.

"You get it all done?" I asked, diverting my attention away from Michael and working to change the mood I was sinking deeply into.

"Finally. Turns out Grace is better than me at changing a tire. She didn't even get dirty," Rob grumbled, walking to the sink and turning on the water.

"I'm efficient and you really did most of the heavy lifting, Rob. I just screwed on the nuts and bolts for you."

"Yeah you did, baby." Rob looked over his shoulder as I bit my tongue. Seth and Michael both shot nasty glares toward my brother.

I laughed and hit my hand on the table. With everything going on it felt good to laugh. "He's kidding!"

Rob sat down beside Grace, moving his chair closer to her just to annoy the boys. Michael moved to the stove.

Seth began divvying out bowls of pasta. "How about we talk about what our plans are from here? We leaving in the middle of the night because it's safer to travel, or are we going to head out in the morning?"

Michael poured sauce onto each bowl. "We'll leave around two. It'll still give us coverage. Some of us can sleep, the others can get things packed and organized."

I reached up and took the bowl from Michael as he offered it, lifting it to my nose and breathing in deeply. Rob did the same when he received his.

Everyone stared at us awkwardly.

"What? We're Grollic. Smells do it for us." Rob shrugged his shoulders and bent over his bowl, his fork moving fast to shovel the hot pasta into his mouth. He didn't seem to mind the burn. I on the other hand would be letting it cool.

"Rouge's not a Grollic." Michael frowned and sat down.

"I'll have to remember that, Rob." Grace flashed a smile at my brother, the grumbles in the room showing disapproval at the continued bantering.

"Let's just go after dinner. I'll drive." I twirled my fork in the bowl and pulled up a heaping portion of pasta, leaning over and nibbling tentatively at it.

"No! There's no way you are driving." Michael caught himself from saying why. "If Grollics or Bentos finds us, we need you rested and ready. Not concentrating on keeping four wheels on the road."

"I'll drive. I'm good and rested." Grace reached for the plate of garlic bread.

Rob took four, where the rest of us took one. I smiled at him as he shrugged sheepishly. How long had he been living the pack life with other males and no one else around him? Rebekah had been dead for at least ten years. Somehow I couldn't picture him without the company of a woman around. I pulled the unused napkin from my lap and offered it to him.

"Thanks." He took it and wiped at his mouth before digging back into his dinner.

Seth grabbed three beers out of the fridge and set them in front of the boys. "Grace is right. She and I can take turns driving tonight. You've been on the run." He leaned back in his chair, reaching to pick up his beer.

"I'm okay with that." Michael nodded, looking over at me and then to my brother. "You guys?"

"Are we taking the Jeep, 'cause that's a tight fit?" Rob looked up, his mouth full of food.

Seth shook his head. "Let's use the Explorer. It's got a third row of seats and room in the back should we need to pick anything up."

"Where are we headed exactly?" I asked, hoping like hell it wasn't Florida. Anywhere but there.

"Florida." Grace pushed her bowl away, hardly nothing having been touched.

"It's our best bet, Rouge." Michael's eyebrows rose as he silently questioned me why it was a bad choice.

Rob shook his head. "I don't know. Florida seems to be a bad place for Grollics. That pack disappeared into thin air down there. It's not safe."

"It's probably the safest. Bentos won't be there," Michael argued. "It's where we have an underground facility. I think it's the best place for us right now. We can't keep running."

"We can't sit still and hope for the best either, right? I thought running was the plan until Jamie, I mean Rouge and I could read the book and figure out what the hell to do." Rob glanced at me for support.

"You can read the book too?" Grace leaned in and stared at Rob.

"Wait. What?" Seth perked up at the end of the table and I wanted to reach over and pop my brother in the back of the head.

"I can't read the journal." Rob shook his head. "But I sure as hell am going to try my best to help Jamie read it."

"It's Rouge!" Michael shouted.

"And you're okay with him helping her?" Seth asked Michael.

I glanced back and forth at the two of them. What weren't they saying?

"Yes," Michael replied. "There are things I'm doing, and things I know, that Caleb isn't aware of." Michael's shoulders visibly stiffened. I reached out and ran my fingers along his thigh, his hand trapping mine and holding me still.

"Ballsy, dude." Seth grinned. "About time you started taking a risk for yourself." He turned his attention back to his bowl.

We all sat in silence for a few minutes, my chest aching with the breath I didn't know I was holding. I let it out slowly as Seth looked back up, his eyes scanning the group before landing on me.

"You don't have to do this with us. Honestly." I smiled at him, trying to offer him the out it seemed like he wanted.

"Are you kidding me? I live for this stuff! I'm looking forward to running for my life, getting physically assaulted by you at least twice a day, and beating some Grollic ass." He glanced at Rob and nodded. "No offense, dude."

"Yeah, yeah," Rob muttered, way more concerned with his dinner than the conversation around him.

"You in?" Michael asked.

"I'm in. Tell me more about what you've learned from the wolf book." He winked at me.

Always the joker. "It's changing. Evolving." I had no idea how to explain it. "It's like someone's inside the book. Like taking a life of its own."

Seth whistled. "Damn! It's like real magic?"

"Real and seemingly alive." Michael turned to face me. "Now it's time to talk."

Chapter 12

"Not if she doesn't want to." Rob looked up, his voice deep with warning.

"It's okay, Rob. Why don't I tell you how I got it, since the others already know most of the back story? I'll keep it short and sweet. I can tell the rest in the car. I want to get out of here. Something's headed this way. It's coming at a much faster rate than we're ready to handle."

Everyone watched me, but no one asked me why I knew that. They seemed to accept whatever was happening to me, could affect them.

"I was working in a small antique shop a while back and found the book. My boss gave it to me. It only caught my attention, it didn't have any powers. Michael saw me with it and that's kind of how we got together." I looked at him and smiled. "Then some crappy stuff happened and I forgot about the book. I found it in my closet and opened it up. I read the history of the Grollics and how this war between the Hunters and Grollics started. I brought the book to Michael and Caleb and found out it wasn't all in English. I see parts as English, I can't explain it. Then when I turned eighteen I gained more knowledge from the journal. I never knew it was Bentos'. We figured out all this stuff together." I glanced around the room at the others, thankful to have them in my life. "What's started happening now, since I met you," I said to Rob, "is beyond what I expected. I figured I'd learn to read the book, find out its secrets. I didn't know I'd opened Pandora's Box." I shrugged and stood, picking up my bowl and walking to dump it in the trash can.

"Where you going with that food?" Rob spoke up, his eyes narrowing slightly.

"I'm done."

Rob gestured with his hand. "Give it here. We're not wasting any food." He gave me his empty one and went back to eating.

"So the book just appeared one day?" Seth hadn't heard the whole story.

"I guess so. Though now understanding better that it's the wolf diary I can say that it would have found me on its own had fate not pushed us together." I leaned over the sink, turning on the water and beginning to wash the empty dishes in preparation for us heading out soon.

"Why would the book find you and not Bentos? He's more powerful than you, right?" Grace asked.

Seth stood and moved to the refrigerator, pulling out a beer and holding it up as I looked at him over my shoulder. "Beer?" he asked and looked around.

"Shouldn't those of you who are driving *not* be drinking?" Rob scoffed.

"Doesn't affect us." Grace smiled as she brushed her fingers past my brother's collar. I turned around fully, leaving the water running.

"Bentos lost the book."

"What?" I blinked, surprised at Rob's words.

"Yeah," he said. "He lost the journal. It's his diary. Maybe someone stole it or tossed it away or something."

"It's old. How long ago did he lose it?"

"He supposedly wrote it when he first found out what he was. Like a journal or memoir. We were told to look for it when it went missing. He lost it about a year or two ago. We looked everywhere. It's like it left the city."

Something about his comments nagged at me. Could that be why I moved with my foster parents? Or that they dumped me in Port Coquitlam? Could they have had the book?

"Don't you think he would be able to read it if he had it?" Seth turned in his seat, his eyes resting on me.

Rob scoffed. "Uh, yeah! The guy wrote it!"

Seth ignored Rob, but his eyes turned bright blue.

We didn't need a fight before we left. I cleared my throat. "Bentos is so much more powerful than me. I've barely scratched the surface on what I know from the book."

"Can you read more than when I saw you last?" Seth asked.

"Only a little bit more. I'm not sure how to harness my power to be able to give myself over to interpret the magic."

"Caleb would know," Seth offered before lifting his hands at the stares he got. "Okay, just saying guys."

"I offered that. She refused." Michael turned and stood up, everyone but Rob now working to clean up. He was busy eating the remains from everyone's bowls. I couldn't help myself but laugh at him. He looked up at me and winked, our relationship already starting to find foundation.

"So you know Bentos had it, Rob?" Grace asked, wiping her hands on a towel and tossing it to Seth.

"He had it." Rob looked up, his humor all but gone.

"How do you know for sure?" I asked, moving toward the table and resting my hands on the back of a chair.

"I saw it when I was younger, one of the few times he visited the house."

"He didn't live with you guys?" Seth asked, moving to stand beside me.

"He didn't live anywhere. He's a bastard that moved around taking what he wanted, women included," Rob responded, sitting back and finally pushing his bowl from in front of him.

The implication was on the table. Bentos had raped their mother and the two of them were products of the man's inability to contain the blackness that had now consumed him. "Now you have his book. Learn to read it." Rob stared at me, his eyes dark.

"It's not that easy." Michael moved up beside him, the growl in his voice less than pleasant.

"You're Hunters, you have no frickin' clue how to read it." There was no joking nature in Rob's voice now.

"And you're a dumb-ass Grollic. The one thing the book is devoted to, killing Grollics." Michael stood, his hard stare not leaving Rob's face.

"And on that note... grab your stuff. We're leaving." Grace moved past us, walking out of the kitchen and forcing us to let things drop where they were and do the same.

"Everyone comfy?" Seth called back to us, the ride having only been a few hours thus far and already I was feeling like I could scratch my skin off.

"No, it's hot and I'm too big for this seat," Rob complained loudly, the light tone of his voice giving off quickly the jesting of his nature.

Grace turned from the passenger seat and smiled flirtatiously at him. "Want to trade me spots?"

"No, but you can come back here with me. I'll make room for ya."

Michael leaned forward and popped Rob on the back of the head, the large Grollic turning and growling softly. "Behave."

"No." Rob smirked and turned back around, repositioning himself to lay across the full bench seat.

"Don't blame you." I leaned back and slid my hand into Michael's, West Virginia having faded in the darkened dust behind us hours ago. I hated running. It felt too much like what I had done most of my life. I wanted to stand and fight, but it wasn't the time yet. I turned on the small light above me and pulled out my personal journal, reading over my entry about the night Michael and I met. The soft sound of him sleeping next to me caused my lip to tug into a smile.

I reached over and brushed the back of my fingers by his cheek, his skin so smooth, almost like silk. To imagine him or Grace having to die to become the incredible beings they were, set fear alive in my heart again. Bentos hadn't known that they were Hunters or he wouldn't have done it, right? I leaned over and pressed a small kiss to Michael's cheek. He didn't need sleep, but could act and function very much like a human. It was a way to pass the long night ahead of them. I would be following suit shortly.

I flipped through the empty pages of my journal, thinking about all of the great times and memories I'd love to fill it with, but nothing was for certain. Not even me and Michael.

The SUV jerked and I sat up, throwing the journal down toward my feet toward my small knapsack. Michael sat up.

"What's the matter?" Rob asked, sitting up out of a dead sleep, his voice thick with dreams.

"Flat tire. Should have had you guys check this vehicle and not the Jeep." Seth adjusted the rear-view mirror, giving a look to what had to be Michael.

"I did what I was told... it's rare and never works out." Rob lifted his hands in the air. "Point and case."

"So dramatic all the time," Michael mumbled as I turned to see the lights of a small convenience store up ahead. Maybe a hundred feet away. So close. I needed to go to the bathroom anyway, so it wasn't such a bad thing.

"Can you make it up to the store so at least I have a little bit of light to change the damn thing?" Rob stretched, his large body taking up the whole area in front of us.

"I have a flashlight in here too. I'll hold it for you if you need me to." Grace turned around and smiled.

I glanced at Michael as I laughed softly. He looked toward me and shook his head as if it were my fault that his sister and my brother got along so well. I shrugged and he mumbled something under his breath. "Caleb's going to skin me."

"This is as far as I can make it, Rob. Sorry buddy." Seth pulled the vehicle off the road and turned to face us. "Grab snacks and go to the restroom?"

"Yeah, I need to go." I moved past Michael, not wanting to wait.

"I'm going to look at the map with Seth. I'll be there in a minute. Be careful." Michael tugged me onto his lap, forcing me to listen. I squirmed and pulled away, my bladder screaming for attention. "I'll watch you from here."

There was no need. It was a stone's throw from the Explorer. I'd be back before Rob had the tire even off. "Yeah, yeah. I doubt any Grollics are hiding out in the ladies room." I huffed and moved past my brother, who had to comment.

"Actually, that's a great place to meet women." Rob popped my leg as I got out of the car. I turned to give him an over exaggerated eye roll, the sound of Grace laughing at him caused me to smile unwillingly.

I walked through the short grassy field, the lights not far ahead of me. Not wanting to take up anyone's time, I picked my walk up to a jog and moved toward the store. I slowed as I approached it and slipped into the air-conditioned building with a sigh. Walking quickly toward the back, I greeted the cashier with a friendly wave and slipped into the bathroom.

Closer...

I washed my hands in the sink before pressing my fingers to my eyes, weariness sitting on me like a well-worn coat.

Closer...

"Closer, what? Who's closer? Where are you?" I spun around the small restroom, the smell of urine making my stomach ache. I needed to get some air and fast.

I pushed open the door and walked out into the empty store, the cashier having disappeared out back.

Closer...

"Stop..." I walked out of the store, the serenity of the night seeming to help a little. I lifted my head to the sky and followed a star as it shot across the sky. A wish was demanded from me.

"I need help. I wish for help. Someone who can assist me. Fix the crazy in my head." A tear rolled down my cheek, my emotions shot from the situation behind me and before me. From wanting Michael so badly and yet not giving myself to him simply because we were damned to never be able to exist as one.

The sound of someone moving to my left caused me to jerk around, the guy before me unknown, but the soft expression on his face said he wasn't a threat.

Too bad he was a Grollic.

Chapter 13

"Don't come a step closer." I lifted my hand, trying hard not to take another step back. I had the ability to protect myself and everyone in the vehicle behind me from hordes of Grollics and yet I couldn't access most of it.

"Who makes a wish and denies its welcome?" He smiled, reaching back and sliding his hand into the back pocket of his jeans. His black t-shirt pulled tight across his chest and abdomen, thick muscles suddenly on display. I jerked my gaze back to his face, not faring much better there.

If Michael was handsome, then Seth was gorgeous. If Seth was gorgeous, this guy was extraordinary. Long dark eyelashes brushed over tanned skin, his eyes the most brilliant amber I had ever seen. His black hair was long enough to hang in his eyes, but cut as such. Nothing about him was shaggy or unkempt. I needed to go.

"I don't know what you're talking about."

"Yes you do."

"Did the vargulf send you?"

A single handsome eyebrow rose. "What?"

The guy didn't have a clue. He probably lived in the dump of a town and had no idea who I was. I glanced over my shoulder. "You need to leave."

"I'm here to help."

"We don't want help."

"Not them. You."

"How do you know me?" I took that damn step back, my resolve crashing in to be brave and bold. He was overwhelming in a good and bad way. My wolf blood felt the truth in his position. He was an Alpha, but whose?

"Your father sent me."

So he did know Bentos. Anger boiled inside of me. I fought to control it. "To kill me?"

"No, to locate you."

"Well, you have. So go back and tell him. Then tell him I hate him, and when he finds me I'll be ready for him." I clenched my teeth as the sound of Rob's voice rose up behind me. He was telling the others I was talking to a stranger.

"You won't be ready." He seemed unperturbed the others could pounce on him at any moment.

"Yes. I will."

"No, but I'll get you ready."

"What?" I didn't understand.

He took another step, his hand moving from his back pocket toward me as if to touch me. I jerked from him, scared at the thought of wanting him to touch me. "Don't come any closer."

"Closer..." he whispered, his eyes darkening as his smile faded. "Only when you ask me to."

I didn't respond. He turned and walked out of the light from the shop. In the darkness he changed into the large beast he was born to be, the back of him long gone before Rob showed up beside me. I turned expecting to see Michael as well.

"Who was that?" Rob asked, breathing in deeply as if trying to get a track on the guy.

"I don't know."

"Flippin' Grollic?"

"Yeah. He said Bentos sent him to locate me."

"And he didn't try to kill you?"

I faced Rob, turning my frustration on him. "Do I look dead?"

He shook his head, knowing better than to make a joke now.

"Did Bentos tell you to kill me when you found me?"

"No. He wants that pleasure for himself I guess."

"Probably. That guy didn't want to kill me either." I looked around to see the rest of our friends laughing by the car. "Michael didn't think to come after me to help?"

"It was one person. I said I could handle it." Rob rolled his shoulder. "We didn't know he was a Grollic."

How could they have missed him? I knew he was wolf immediately.

"You okay?"

"Yeah... I guess." I turned and walked back to the car, a little surprised that Michael didn't come to me when he saw the guy approach me. Maybe he didn't see it.

Who was the guy? Was he the one whispering *closer* to me? I reached up and rubbed my fingers along my eyebrows, pressing my face into my hands as the world got more confusing.

Michael moved toward me. "What did that guy want from you?"

"Don't know." I shrugged and moved to the car. I was ticked my protector hadn't bothered to show up. "I'm not feeling well. Okay if I ride shotgun for a while?"

"I'll drive," Grace piped up. We looked over at Seth who was still running his finger along a large map. He nodded and I got in the car, rolling down the window. I couldn't get the image of the stranger out of my head.

"You okay?"

I started to say I was fine but caught myself. "Did you realize that guy was a Grollic?"

Michael's eyes went big and then burned bright. "What?" He jerked his head back to the direction where I had been talking to the stranger.

"He told me Bentos sent him to find us." I buckled up and leaned back, the expression on Michael's face hardening.

"Why the hell did you let him go?"

"I can't explain it." I shrugged.

"Well try." Michael's voice dropped an octave, his voice filling with irritation.

I leaned toward the window and bent down to press my lips to his. "No. It's too convoluted. If we think that Bentos doesn't already know exactly where we are, then we are the idiots."

Rob patted the side of the SUV. "Let's get this bird in motion. Seems like we've been spotted by the enemy. I'm sure we've got one hell of a fight coming our way."

Seth folded the map and him and Rob got in the back. Rob took the last row and stretched out.

I patted Michael's arm, not entirely sure how to calm him down. "The Grollic was meant to be a threat, for sure, but offing him simply because he was being controlled to find us? I couldn't do it," I tried to explain to Michael, and to myself. "He didn't try to kill us."

Michael frowned. "Bentos finding us was inevitable."

"I didn't realize what was happening until it was over. He just wanted to talk."

Michael's frown deepened. "You're turning toward them, Rouge. They're killers, abominations. They have to die." He moved back as sadness rushed through me.

"Then I should too." I rolled up the window and turned around, the stern look of warning on his features too much for me to handle.

I closed my eyes, the soft touch of Grace's fingers brushing by my arm causing me to turn to look at her.

"You okay?" she whispered, starting the car and pulling out as soon as Michael's door shut.

"Yeah. Just too much lately." I looked out the side window, trying to make out the figure of a lone wolf. I didn't need another man in my life, but what if somehow he had been sent to help, to really help?

I had just wished upon that star and then he showed up? Coincidence? Was anything lately?

"Want to talk about it?" Grace asked softly.

"No. Too many testosterone ears in this place." I pulled my legs up to my chest and wrapped my arms around them, leaning back and resting as best I could. The new Grollic-guy seemed to be on my side, not Bentos'. He hadn't even told me his name.

Probably for the best.

Guilt washed over me for wanting to know it. I needed to wrap up beside Michael and remember who I was, but... who was that?

"Something happen between you and my brother?" Grace asked, not seeming to want to let the conversation go.

"No. I'm just trying to figure out what to do about this fight, and how to protect everyone that I love in the midst of it."

"You don't need to protect us, Rouge. And you're not alone."

"Am I not?" I pressed my forehead against the cold glass and let out a long sigh. "Grollics are an abomination like Michael just said. If that's so, then I'm the mother lode of that."

"You're not a Grollic. You're different."

I scoffed, turning to look at my closest friend. "A frog is born a frog and can never be changed into anything else."

"Not so."

I shook my head. "It starts out as a tadpole but it always changes into a frog. Always."

"In the movies if a pretty girl kisses the frog he sometimes becomes a prince."

"Or she gets warts on her mouth," Rob yelled from the back seat.

"Gross..." I muttered as Grace laughed. She was really taking a liking to him.

"People can change, Rouge," Grace said quietly. "Don't give up on that. It's like leaving hope in the dust."

"I can change my clothes, my hair, my voice, wear colored contacts and even push my attitude and persona to shift..." I let out a long sigh, knowing Michael was listening to us. "But I'll always be the Seventh Mark. Grollic blood flows in me. Nothing else." I sighed long and hard, staring out at the passing dark scenery. "It seems like I should start trying to embrace that."

Something enormous hit the top of the car suddenly. I screamed. The serenity of being in a low-key conversation with Grace shattered violently.

"Something's after us," Grace yelled as the boys moved into action. I turned to see Michael swing open the door to the SUV and crawl out, Seth going behind him.

"Slow the car!" I yelled as Grace sped up.

"No! Look behind us! Hell's hounds! There must be a hundred of them."

"Wow... that's some shit there." Rob's voice was almost playful. He cracked his knuckles and stretched his neck out.

"Slow down and let me out. I'll stop them." I moved to grab the handle to the car, Grace stopped me, moving much faster as she grabbed me and pulled back hard.

"You can do whatever you do from the seat here. You don't need to stop, drop and die."

The fighting above us scared me to death. We were going much too fast for anyone to be on top of the SUV. A hairy body flew off the side of the car and fell to the side of the road.

Michael crawled in, grumbling loudly.

"Where's Seth?" I asked, turning around in my seat as my heart beat wildly. I wanted to crawl over to him and kiss him. I checked to see if he'd been bit.

"He's beating the beast senseless."

Beast...

"You should have killed that bastard back at the gas station. This was his doing."

Grace and I screamed as the large body of the Grollic rolled down the front window and off the hood. The SUV almost catching wind as we ran over his enormous body. I grabbed the dashboard as Seth slid back in the car, a smile on his handsome face.

"That was fun! Best part was riding the wave of you guys running him over." He laughed and looked back at Rob. "You missed it, dude."

"Yeah... next time. Or better yet, probably this time." His smile faded. He didn't seem too happy to have to kill his own kind.

"We can drive faster than they can run, we'll just go until we run out of gas. Then we can stop and fight." Seth turned in his seat, his face registering shock as well. Michael sat with his head back, his eyes closed. I turned in time to hear Grace whisper a curse.

A line of massive beast bodies stood on the street just in front of us. Grace slammed on the brakes, their ability to run over one or two doable, but ten of them would tear the Explorer in half.

I reached for the door and slid out as everyone in the car screamed for me to get back in. I stomped quickly toward them, looking for the one that had stood before me and lied only moments ago. What was the point? What did he mean to prove?

"Where are you?" I screamed, realizing I didn't know his name. The large horde of beasts behind us growled out and I turned, lifting my hands in the air and screaming in a language I didn't understand, my sense of self-preservation lost to the darkness that pushed against my vision. They stopped in place, frozen in time. My friends piled out of the car and I yelled for them to stop as well, all of them staying still as I turned back to the remaining ten who were left with free will. They growled at me, their jowls bloody and dripping slobber.

I'd never known I'd controlled them and now I didn't know what I was saying to them? What the hell was happening to me? Anger burned deep inside my belly, growing and hardening into pure hatred.

"Closer... I want you to come closer to me," I whispered, not sure if it would work. The large wolf at the front morphed and moved toward me, the boy from the store naked, bare and proud.

"Only since you're asking." His lip lifted in a smile as he stopped in front of me.

"Rouge. What're you doing?" Michael's voice resounded behind me, but I ignored him.

"Does he not know?" The male looked around me, his eyes narrowing on my friends.

"Are you here to help me or hurt me?" I demanded.

"Help you."

"Then why all of this?"

"To show you who I am."

"Make them leave."

"Release them from your hold, witch, then I will."

"I'm no witch." I turned and lifted my voice toward the dark sky, the hundreds of Grollics sinking toward the ground. Forced to stay dormant and lay on the ground. I shuddered to think I could kill them all without them doing anything.

The lone Grollic left standing made a noise at the back of his throat. "Go to Florida. I'll find you there," he whispered behind me. "We'll be together."

My eyes locked onto Michael's, his eyes radiant blue. Confusion covered his handsome features.

"I'm not interested." The Grollic stayed in place only because I forced him to. I turned. "I don't want you to find me. I'm taken and I'll stay that way."

"I'm Joshua, Miss Taken and I agree. You very much belong to me. Make sure your boyfriend understands so I don't have to kill him later."

"Never," I whispered, the fight leaving my voice as I felt myself being tugged toward him by something almost unseen.

"You want the key to beating your father, Jamie?"

"I know the key."

"You understand the power of three?"

"I'm working on it."

"Bentos will kill you and all your friends if you don't find the answer."

Like I didn't know that already. "Who are you?"

"I already told you that. Now, go to Florida and listen for me when the book calls you to. I'll tell you what the three things are because you belong to me."

"I do not." I took a step back as he took one forward. He could move against my control?

"Rouge." Michael's voice lifted again, the anger in it almost scaring me.

"Deny it and I'll not come near you again."

Closer.

"I can't." I turned and walked back toward my friends as Joshua changed back into the wolf, his cry lifting into the sky, the power in it disbursing all of the Grollics to disappear from their sight.

I reached Michael who pulled me close. "What the hell was that?"

It didn't make sense, but I began to see a glimmer of something. Hope? "A friend, I think."

Chapter 14

Rob cleared his throat. "Um, yeah. I don't know who your other friends are, but when someone sends a horde of angry wolves after me, I'm not thinking they're a friend. We call that foe where I'm from." He moved close, but stood out of arm's reach as if scared I might hurt him.

"I think he's trying to help me."

"Do you know him from your past? Something you're not telling me?" Michael spoke through clenched teeth, his eyes lighting up the space in front of him with their brilliance.

I didn't want him hurt. He was my future, all that I wanted in my life. I slipped my hand into his and pulled in closely to him. "No! I just met him, but he's promising to help us. He seems to want Bentos dead and gone as much as we do. I'm sure he's sick of being controlled by him. I'm supposed to be the only thing that can stop him. It's a viable option." I shrugged as he glared down at me.

"And he would rather be controlled by you?" Michael bit back. "Maybe that's what he's looking for – a female Alpha just for himself."

I climbed in the back of the Explorer now covered in scratches and dents and motioned for him to come with me. He stood frozen until Rob poked him in the back. Reluctantly he crawled into the car and sat beside me. I moved toward him, sliding my hand into his and pressing my cheek to his shoulder. "I'm not trying to control anyone. I'm trying not to use my power. Every time I do I send off a flare for Bentos."

"And you don't think what this guy just caused you to do sent over a whole fireworks show?" Michael scoffed, his tone demeaning and hurt.

"Of bloody course it did! I bet he's trying to show his power as an Alpha, Michael. He doesn't control his pack, but he sure as crap had a very large one following him. Have you ever seen anything like that?"

Michael gave a curt shake of his head.

"If that's his army, and Bentos has a larger one, we're screwed. Or if we can use his army against Bentos, we might have a fighting chance. Maybe I'm the lesser of the evils in this world."

I pulled from him as Rob turned around in the seat in front of us. "She has a point. I don't like it either, but being controlled by another person, especially one with nefarious intent is worse than walking through hell." Rob shrugged but didn't turn around.

"Nice choice of words. Made you sound uber-intelligent," Seth piped up from the front seat.

"Thanks, man. I try. I try. I didn't get the fancy ed-du-cation you Hunter folks got all the time for. Once around the sun man, that's all I have."

Seth chuckled. "Once around the sun is a year, dummy."

I rolled my eyes, and then stared out the window by Michael so I could see him as well. "This place in Florida, is it a stronghold? Could it protect us?"

"It's a fortress. I helped build it." Seth elbowed Grace. "Wait till I show you my lair."

I ignored their banter and hoped we could just get to Florida without ten more stops where anything and everything came pounding out of the forest to devour us. The stranger threw me. It was like he was trying to court me cave-man style. I shook my head trying to clear the confusion. I sure as heck didn't belong to the wolf behind us in the woods, but I wasn't so sure I belonged to the man next to me. I loved him, but to what cost?

What would he be willing to sacrifice for us? He said everything and yet every other utterance from him was so derogatory toward my kind. How long before he finally admitted I was a Grollic? How long before he began to hate who I was inside? The Grollic blood was mine now and forever. I couldn't change that.

I finally let it all go, the need for sleep leaving me achy and angry over things I had yet learned to control. I was tired of thinking and sleep seemed the only way out of it.

"Rouge, wake up. We're almost there." Michael shook my shoulder, his voice next to my ear as he leaned against me. Guess a night of not talking calmed his jealous anger toward me.

"Almost there? We were nine hours away when we got back after..." I let my sentence trail off, not wanting to bring the Grollic Joshua up.

"Yep. You've been out like someone drugged your ass. You all right?" Rob turned around, his smile reaching from ear to ear. His hair was a mess and I couldn't help myself from reaching up and trying to fix it.

Michael tugged at my arm, rolling his eyes at me. He was moody... fantastic.

"Leave him be. Nothing you can do with that mop."

I pulled from him and leaned over, reaching up and brushing Rob's hair with my fingers again. He stuck his tongue out at Michael. I swatted the back of his head. So much for trying. "I really slept for nine hours?" I yawned, which felt ridiculous, but too much sleep was sometimes as bad as not enough.

"You did." Grace now sat in the passenger seat beside Seth who was driving. Rob shifted to face her, Grace's smile widening a little. I'd have to ask her what was up with them when Michael wasn't around. I glanced over at him to see if holding his hand was a possibility. Nope. He was pissy at best and I wasn't in the mood.

I ran my fingers over his Siorghra necklace that sat around my neck. I was almost surprised Rob hadn't asked me about it yet, but he seemed to be wise beyond his years. He most likely understood very well what it meant. I leaned forward and laid my cheek on the top of the bench seat in front of me.

Rob glanced at me from the side. "What's up?"

"Do you know what this is?" I held it up.

He looked away, as if annoyed it was on my neck, finally he nodded. "Of course. It's a ball and chain."

I rolled my eyes and Michael huffed beside me. For having angel blood inside of him, he sure spent a lot of his time acting like an ass. Must be his dark side.

"Hunters share these with those they plan to spend forever with. Do Grollics have something similar?"

"It's not an external sign like that. It's internal." Rob shrugged as if the idea of bonding with another held no desire for him.

"Explain."

Michael sat up, taking my attention and pulling the conversation toward him. "Supposedly, the Grollics have mating in their DNA."

I glanced at him in surprise. I had no idea. Not that the conversation had ever come up to talk about.

"We do like the hump-n-bump." Rob lifted his hands in the air and danced a little. I laughed as Grace looked around and wagged her eyebrows.

Michael watched them and then continued. "Each wolf has a mate created for them and when they find that special hairy beast to share forever with, their hearts are as much connected internally as what we would consider with our Siorghra necklaces."

"And it just happens? You just meet that special wolf one day and boom?" I clapped my hands together for effect. It sounded a lot like Hunters.

Rob turned and lifted his eyebrow at Michael. "How about you let a Grollic tell it? Like listening to someone who's never gotten drunk describe being a lush."

"Whatever..." Michael turned and looked out the window as Seth moved the car toward a large ten-foot iron gate. I leaned to look out my window, the property just beyond the gate nothing more than an acre of land. There was a small building sitting in the middle of it, but nothing else other than the fence.

"When you find that someone they are the opposite of you. Where he's bossy and controlling, you're docile and kind. Where you're angry and have fits of rage, he soothes you." Rob shrugged. "The mating doesn't take effect usually until you make love the first time, but... in stronger bonds it can happen sooner."

"And what happens if you mate with a Grollic?" I turned from the window as Michael coughed loudly. My eyes moved to him. "What? I'm just curious."

"But why are you curious? This has nothing to do with you."

"It has everything to do with me. I'm not interested in mating with anyone, but I want to know what happens to the people I belong to, what happens to my brother." I narrowed my eyes at him. I lowered my voice, "You'd better get in a decent mood. I'm tired of this walking on eggshells around you."

"Me too," Rob added.

"She's right. You're being an ass," Grace called from the front as Michael shrugged.

Rob must have sensed the tension and decided to take the stage to give Michael some space. "You want me to tell you about the birds and the bees? What sex is?" He puffed his chest. "Or how real men do it. Grollics, that is."

"No... Please no." Seth turned and chuckled, all of us except Michael breaking into a chuckle. He held his resolve, his arms moving to tightly wrap around his chest.

Seth stopped the car and we all piled out. I moved near Rob, still curious what he had to say.

"I've mated with female Grollics, but I haven't found my match yet, I guess." He moved to help grab our bags out and walked toward the small shack ahead of us.

Worry creeped up inside of me. There wasn't much in the way of coverage around us and the beach sat just a stone's throw away from the small structure. I'd have to ask Rob about the whole linking of the DNA thing another time. It seemed too similar to Hunters. It's a shame the two races couldn't get along as they might actually see how good it could be.

"It's an elevator. Stop worrying." Michael moved past me, his words for me, but his eyes not giving me a second glance.

"Hey Robbo," Seth said, trying to sound jovial but I sensed a deeper undertone in his voice. "If you mate with a Grollic and she dies, do you feel that loss forever? Is your heart broken for all of time until you die too?"

"I don't know myself. But a part of you dies with her. Some even die then and there. If the bond is too strong. Some are asses and have no respect for women. Some..." Rob lugged his bag over his shoulder and nodded. "We can talk later. Mister-I'm-in-charge is getting his panties in a wad. No more talking about doing the dirty with a wolf-man for you, Missy." He ruffled my hair.

I laughed and Grace did as well, moving to walk on the other side of Rob.

"I'd like to talk a little more about that subject," she whispered, probably not thinking I would hear. She winked at him as Rob's shoulders stiffened.

His grin turned wickedly sly. "Would you now?" His voice dropped slightly, the sound of it almost attractive.

"I can still hear you guys." Michael turned back to pin us with a healthy dose of 'shut the hell up'. "Cut it out now." He pointed at Rob. "You are *not* touching my sister."

"I don't care what you hear." Grace moved up and pressed the numbers on the keypad, turning and motioning for Seth. "We have to get everything in fast. The door can only be opened for a minute before the alarm starts going off. It's highly secure here, so we should be good."

"So that's why the shack. Rob whistled. "Hide the truth."

"It's an elevator down to the facility." Michael moved to open the door, walking in first and almost letting it shut behind him.

I growled softly, so tired of his moods and yet unable to offer him anything but more worry and more angst. Maybe he was struggling with something he wasn't telling me. That would be nothing new to call home about.

"I'm coming, sorry." Seth jogged up, his handsome face filled with mischief. "I am so going skinny dipping in that water."

"There might be sharks... or piranhas." I walked into the small hallway.

Michael frowned, leaning out of the elevator with a pensive look on his face.

"Sharks maybe, but nothing else. I doubt a shark is going to swim in the shallow parts of the ocean." Seth laughed and moved into the small elevator as we all squeezed in tightly. He stood in front of me, looking down and smiling.

"I'll go." I could be dead when this was all over. What if I never got the chance again to skinny dip? The way things were between Michael and me, it might be the only fun I'd ever have again.

"No you won't," Michael responded, shaking his head as I looked back at him.

I turned and looked up at Seth winking and mouthing, "I'll go."

Seth chuckled and quickly made his expression unreadable as he looked back at Michael. "What's up with you? The lack of fighting earlier on the trip leave you restless and needing to let off some steam?"

"My life leaves me restless."

I turned to see what expression accompanied his truth, but got nothing. He closed his eyes and laid his head back, the elevator stopping before I asked.

"We each get our own room. Get off..." Michael muttered and moved past me toward the hall.

He was pissed and I wasn't exactly sure why. What had I done now?

The scary part was, I wasn't sure if I cared at the moment.

Chapter 15

The rooms were small... too small. No windows because we were too far underground. Not even a picture to pretend with. Just bricks. I could feel the walls closing in on me and it wasn't more than fifteen minutes after sitting I wanted to head back outside. It was mid-day and the others would most likely be eating lunch. My stomach hurt due to the stress of trying to figure out what part this new Grollic played in my fight against Bentos.

Michael was upset. Could it be because of my unwillingness to have him fight the night before? It annoyed me if that was the reason. All those Grollics, we wouldn't have stood a chance if I hadn't stepped up. At least that's what I told myself.

I pulled my suitcase off the bed and dropped my journal on my pillow. A reminder to write in it later in hopes that it might help me think through where things were and how to push them further – in the right direction.

I slipped the wolf journal under my t-shirt, tucking it in the back of my jeans and letting my shirt cover it. I didn't want the pressure of everyone in the whole compound expecting me to understand it.

I left my room and hesitated by the door I'd seen Michael disappear into earlier, my hand pressing to the cold metal. I should ask him to come with me. His pride had just been hurt... right?

Nothing had ever been straightforward between us. I turned and walked away quickly, sighing heavily. He loved me and I loved him, but maybe love wasn't enough. We had thought it would be, but that was naive thinking. My fingers brushed over his Siorghra, the smooth surface becoming something of familiarity to me. The book at my back heated slightly, a word whispering through my mind again.

Closer.

I didn't understand. How did Joshua know I had the journal? Was it the book or him who was able to speak in my mind? It couldn't be him. He was a Grollic. Bentos must have told him I had it.

It wasn't the book talking, but the inherent power that lay within its pages. Evil and ancient mystery birthing something so fundamental in its creation that it held immense power.

It heated more and I pulled it from my back as I slipped into the elevator. When the doors closed I realized I had no idea what the code was to get back in, but the metal contraption was already headed up. Hopefully Seth decided to go skinny dipping. I kind of didn't care if I ended up trapped outside. Anything was better than being stuck underground right now.

I fanned the book, my heart beating a little too fast for comfort as the journal cooled slightly, as if understanding my desires. I stared at it. Was that possible?

The door to the elevator opened and I walked out into the early afternoon sunlight, the breeze from the ocean cool, the sun hot. I rolled up my sleeves, shifting the journal from hand to hand until I felt a little more prepared to bake in the sun. I headed to the water where the long stretch of beach lay empty of people.

"Good," I whispered and walked to my left until I couldn't see where I came from or where I was going. I moved back to the edge of the sand, large palm trees providing a little bit of shade if you sat directly underneath them. I slipped my shoes off, my calves tired from walking through the sand. I sat down, pulling the journal up to my view line and opening it.

"Just open your truths to me, and let me be strong enough to handle them." I flipped to the page with the triangle, Rob's assessment of the power leading me to believe it was three people that we needed, but who? Not three items of power, but three people.

I ran my finger over the symbol. Nothing. Sighing softly, I flipped back through more pages and stopped on the Grollic symbol, the one on my shoulder blade but shown on the front of the Grollic in the hand drawn picture. The mark was always confusing me.

A strange thought hit me. How jacked up was the universe that it would give Bentos a daughter instead of a son. The seventh son, wasn't that the folklore? The seventh was given the name Benjamin to ward off the Grollic ability. Rob called me Jamie – which could be short for Benjamin.

When the seventh son was born, did that shift of power start immediately or not until they turned the age of shifting?

"You look like you're deep in thought."

I turned and covered the top of my eyes with my hand, the voice familiar and not.

Joshua.

"What're you doing here?"

"Same as you."

"What am I doing here?"

"Looking for answers I suppose." He smiled.

I swear my heart melted a little. I forced it to harden and just use my head to think with.

"Can I?" He pointed to the spot in the shade next to me.

I glanced down at it, contemplating whether it was a good idea to let him anywhere near me. How would I feel if a Hunter appeared out of nowhere and wanted Michael's attention? A really good looking Hunter?

"Sure. It's a free beach." I shrugged and moved over a safe distance as he sat down next to me.

He reached over and I quickly pulled the book out of his reach. He didn't take it from me. "May I?"

"You can try." I chuckled, waiting in morbid curiosity to see him yelp in pain as the book burnt him like it had Rob.

He smiled, his eyes moving across my face as if memorizing it. He was different, scary and dominant, but something in his demeanor screamed peace at me. He took the book and flipped to the page with the power of three.

Shoot. So much for being the smart one. I was always ready to protect this book with my life, and now I'd just basically given it to the enemy. I was an idiot! "It's not hot?"

"No. Should it be?" His white t-shirt brought out the tan of his skin, his shorts fitting him a little too well.

"I thought all Grollics couldn't touch it. Just me. And Bentos."

"Ahhh. It finds me familiar because of our link." He glanced at me and shrugged before looking down, his brow squinting. "I wish I could read it though."

"Our familiarity?" I asked, my voice a little too light and airy. I almost could touch the truth of his words, but didn't want to dive off that cliff. Scared as hell, I moved a little, turning to face him and crossing my legs in the sand.

"Can you read it?" He handed it back to me.

I pulled it a little too quickly to appear un-phased from giving it to him a minute ago.

"Look at the power of three. Can you tell me if you understand the wolf-speak?"

I grinned. *Wolf-speak?* It sounded better than 'foreign language'. His finger brushed mine as he pointed. A sharp prick of electricity rushed through my fingertips. I gasped.

He lifted his eyebrow as if trying to figure me out.

I stared down at the book, not wanting to show the vulnerability I know was showing in my eyes. Words blurred on the page of the book, my chest hurting as the air thickened.

Joshua reached out and touched my knee, his words commanding. "Don't let the magic own you, Jamie. You own it."

I had no idea what he meant, but I pressed on, the words making sense only for a moment. Gasping, I looked up, the beach behind him now covered in dark clouds.

"Incredible." He reached out and touched my cheek, his fingers brushing along the side of my face. "The color of your eyes shifted due to the power of the book."

"It's the Siorghra, the journal and the Seventh Mark." Rob had been wrong. We didn't need people, we needed objects. "They're all intertwined with magic."

He smiled and shook his head. "Beautifully done. You have all of those things?"

I touched Michael's necklace, his lifeblood. "I can't use Michael's Siorghra. I can't let anything happen to it." It wasn't mine to take.

"Michael? The Hunter helping you?"

"My boyfriend."

He chuckled. "But you're a Grollic. You can't be with a Hunter." He moved his hand from me as my hand dropped from the top of his. I didn't remember reaching out to touch him.

"I'm not sure what I am." I let out a long sigh and stood. I shouldn't be telling him such intimate information.

"Listen to me. I know you don't know me yet, but you will. I've been sent to take you to Bentos. However I hate him more than you do, rest assured. You're not going to have the luxury of waiting for him to find you. You need to move fast. People are dying and he's only getting stronger."

"I thought he was getting weaker." *Because of my growing ability.*

"You've barely touched the edge of your power. He would destroy you."

"Then I can't call him to me. That makes no sense. It'll be a massacre."

"No it won't. My pack's enormous and we'll stand with you."

"He can control you and every other Grollic."

"Not if you take ownership first. If you control us then he cannot remove that ownership without killing you."

Was that true? It had to be. Instinct told me he was right. "Why are you doing this?"

Joshua stood and took a step toward me, the large male outweighing Michael and my brother by thirty pounds at least.

"Because our future is linked. I have seen it."

"Are you a witch?" The immediate familiarity with him left my mind spinning. It almost felt like I'd known him half my life.

"No, but I think you'll find that you're far more than a Grollic."

"How do you know this?"

"My mother was a special lady. I know a lot of things." He smiled and reached toward me. I moved a step closer, wanting his hand to brush by my skin. Shame should have rushed in at my thought and feelings, but it didn't. I was grateful for the moment for I knew it would come soon.

"You have to take ownership of us, Jamie. And then you call Bentos to you and bring your friends in for the battle."

"When?"

"Late tonight."

"No. There's no way."

"We have the perfect weapon to use to kill Bentos where he stands."

"The journal?" Maybe there was deep magic inside of it. Maybe Bentos had a witch use dark magic to protect it. If there were Grollics and Hunters, why couldn't there be powerful witches?

"You." He reached out and brushed his fingers down my neck, the tingles burning my skin in a way that left me breathless.

"Me?" I pulled back, my eyes widening as the sun moved behind the clouds. "I'm not ready for this. My ability is uneven, unusable. I can't control it. I'll end up killing you and half your pack."

"No, you won't."

"I can't even read this damn book." I held it up and growled softly. It burned as if angry at me.

"You just did."

"Yeah, because you told me to." I rolled my eyes at how ridiculous that sounded, but it was true, wasn't it?

"Because of our connection."

He said it again and I felt it rush over me.

Closer.

I wanted to step closer, but I knew it would change everything if I did. I forced myself to take a step back, reaching to tuck the book in the back of my pants.

"I need time to think. I have to talk to Michael." *My boyfriend. The love of my life who would risk anything and everything for me.*

"I understand. I'll be waiting here just after sundown. If you want us to fight with you, come to me and make me yours. Then he cannot have us."

Bentos? "And how do I call Bentos to us if we decide to do this?" Kind of an important question to know the answer to.

"The book has that spell."

I flipped it open and bent my head to the side, flipping through it I wondered what Joshua meant by making him mine. Did he mean taking control of his Grollic form... or something more?

He reached out and touched one of the last pages in the book, a large serpent painted across the top. I had never noticed it before, and I'd gone through the book a lot. Had it been there all along? "That will call him."

"How..." I stopped myself from asking, knowing that if I was going to even consider this, I needed to get everyone on board with it. I stared at the page and then squinted as I tried to get the language to make sense, but nothing. I glanced up and let out a frustrated sigh.

Joshua smirked, his features so regal and breathtaking. "I'm going to walk around you and hold you as you try again."

"What? No!"

"Trust me. Just let me try it. I'm not working to seduce you... yet." He laughed.

I felt my heart shudder. I needed to go. This was stupid and dangerous. He could snap my neck and kill me. "Fine. Hold me loosely. Nothing intimate." What the heck was I doing?

He moved behind me as my body stiffened automatically, fear rushing around my heart. It felt like treachery, like I was pulling out a long knife and preparing to stab Michael in the heart. Joshua slid his arms around me, his large chest pressed to my back and the word blurred a little as I sunk against him.

He leaned down and pressed his face to the side of mine, my breath catching in my lungs as my hands trembled slightly. "Read it, Jamie. Don't concentrate on me. I'm the calm to your storm, the wind to your fire. Rest against me and open yourself up. Be who you were born to be and let me contain the power. I won't let it overflow or scare you. I'll help you control it."

I murmured as I tried to read the page, reaching back with one hand and running my fingers through his hair as I tried to pull him closer, the need to nuzzle against him causing my stomach to contract, my heart to ache. Why was I touching him? *Focus, Rouge! Just get what you need from the journal, whatever it takes!*

"Read it... not out loud, but see that it's me who allows you to be who you really are."

I stared down at the page, not sure what he meant, but believing him. The words shuffled and changed. Plain English suddenly laying in front of me. Before I realized what I was doing I closed my eyes, the incantation lifting from my lips.

"From the north and south bring the power of three.

As you rise from the valley, come and stand before me.

Try and take what is mine as the world becomes dark,

For the father shall die and awake the Seventh Mark."

I could hear Joshua yelling for me to stop, but I couldn't seem to stop the rhythm of the poem. The clouds above us closed in, darkness shrouding the sky. I turned as he leaned in, his hands gripping my shoulders hard.

"You have to go!" he hissed. "Bentos is coming now! You've got maybe twelve hours before he's here. He's coming straight for you, Jamie. Shit." He leaned in and pulled me toward him, his lips pressing against mine as he whispered against my mouth.

My hands pressed against his chest, ready to push him away but I didn't.

"Take me!" he whispered hoarsely. "Take me and seal this fight for us." He kissed me again as rain began to pour from the darkened day. The world shifted around us and I reached out, clinging to him in complete confidence.

I suddenly knew the words I needed to say. "You are mine, as is your pack. Get them together and prepare. This is going to be one heck of a battle." I moved past him, tucking the journal in my shirt as I started to run, something feeling so right about what I had begun. Power pulsed through me, my skin alive with the rush of the wind, my eyes seeing so much more than I had before.

I needed to talk to Michael. We had to stand as a united force. *Even when you've just betrayed him?*

I had no idea the part Joshua would play in my future, but for tonight, he and his Grollics would be my soldiers and I would be their Alpha. I sped up my pace, excited by the thought.

Chapter 16

Grace stood waiting for me by the compound door as I ran back. Her arms crossed over her chest, one knee bent with her foot resting against the brick. She stared at me through her sunglasses even though I couldn't see her eyes. "Out for a run?" She straightened and turned to punch the code to get back inside.

"Yeah." I panted from the sprint back from the beach. "Sort of."

We rode down in silence. I had no idea what she had seen or if she had just been looking for me. I assumed with her crazy-good hearing she had heard more than she wanted to. She seemed mad but I had too much on my plate to worry about it right now.

"What just happened?" Rob stood waiting when the metal door slipped open and I stepped out of the elevator bank. I felt numbed by the last few minutes, the distinct taste of dark power from the journal still sitting on me. My stomach felt ready to heave with nothing inside of it. He took my shoulders in his hands, concern sweeping across his handsome features.

"I read a part of the journal I couldn't before."

"That's not all you read," Grace mumbled.

"What part?" Rob didn't even notice Grace behind me. "You did something, we could all feel it down here."

"You could feel it?"

"You'd have to be dead not to feel the shockwave of whatever happened." Rob nodded toward Grace. "She went tearing up to get you." He shook his head. "It was like a wave of darkness rolling over me. That moment in a scary movie when you know the shit is going to hit the fan."

I wanted to laugh or roll my eyes, but I couldn't seem to move past the shock that weighed heavy on me. I could hear my own breathing, slow and steady, back to normal even after running. It gave no credence to the storm deep inside me. Had Joshua really pulled that power from me or was it that he steadied me enough to let me find it myself?

"What happened, Rouge?" Grace asked.

I glanced at my best friend and then to Rob, forcing my focus on him so I could concentrate. "I read a summoning for Bentos."

"What?" Grace cried out.

"It's time to stand against him."

"We just got here! How do you know you're even ready?" Grace began to pace the small hallway.

Rob moved and reached for her. "It's time. Rouge's ready."

I tried to smile and appear confident. "I guess I am."

"When's he coming?" Grace asked at the same time Rob asked, "Did you figure out what the power of three is?"

"It's the Siorgha, the journal and... me." I ran my tongue over my lips, my mouth dry. "I need some water." The room began to spin and I reached for the wall to steady myself. Eyes half closed, I mumbled, "I'm not feeling so well."

Rob put his arm around my waist. "Go get Michael," he told Grace. "I'll help Rouge to her room." When Grace ran down the hall, Rob leaned close to me and helped me walk. "Is that Grollic involved in your decision to call out Bentos?"

I paused when we reached my bedroom door, trying to work through the implication of my answer. I inhaled slowly and glanced over my shoulder at my brother. "Yeah. He's the Alpha of that large pack from before. They'll be here at sundown to fight alongside us."

Rob jerked his fingers through his hair. "Bentos'll take over all of them. You're putting a death warrant on everyone!" He punched the brick wall. "Jamie, I believe in you, but this is crazy!"

"We have to do it now." I inhaled, hating that the air felt stale and smelled like dirt. "I claimed Joshua and his pack for my own. I have them on my side."

"You're sure of that? You sure this Joshua dude isn't screwing you over? He could be one of Bentos' soldiers."

"He's not!" I didn't doubt myself, even if all the others thought so. "I control Joshua and his pack. Bentos won't be able to get them back."

He stared at me. "You sure about this?"

"Positive." I wish I felt as sure as my voice sounded.

"Then I'll gather everyone together."

"You're not mad?" I reached out and wrapped my fingers around the icy cold door handle.

"I want this shit over as much as you do. Running has never been my style."

"Mine either. Nor Michael's." I forced a smile. "We haven't really been running though, have we? Let's kick some Grollic butt."

He shook his head. "Please don't say that on the battlefield. No one's going to follow you to war with a sweet talking mouth like that." He hurried down the corridor.

I watched him disappear around the corner before I opened the door to my room. Inside I yelped when I saw Michael standing by my bed.

He didn't look up or even notice me in the room. That seemed impossible with his hearing ability. I watched from the door, my eyes going from his face down to his hands. My diary lay in them as he flipped through the pages, his face distorted in disgust.

"Hey!" I stopped on the other side of the bed and waited for him to look up. When he did I didn't much like what I saw.

His eyes were bright as if blue fire lit them from behind. His face was solemn, but the purse of his lips told me he was more ticked than before, and once again I was the cause of it. "Why didn't you tell me about this?" He tossed the diary at me.

I caught it and glared back at him. "It's a diary. What business is it of yours to read it? It's personal!" I dropped the wolf journal on the bed with my diary before setting both hands on my hips.

When he didn't say anything I pushed further.

"You knew I bought it to start writing in it! *We* thought it would be good for me. I haven't put anything that's secretive, but it's my personal thoughts." I couldn't remember what I might've written that would make him this angry.

"Stop jacking around and tell me why you didn't tell me about the journal!" His hands shook as he gestured with them.

I grabbed the diary and flipped to a written page, the reality no different than what I had just said. "You want me to narrate it to you?" I glanced at my written words. "This page describes how much I love you. How I'm terrified you are going to leave me. How I think I'm the one thing that could destroy you! That I hate who I am, what I am!" Tears threatened to fall but I refused to let them leave my eyes. I threw the journal at him and grabbed clean clothes out of the bag near the bed. I pulled my shirt over my head before turning and pulling my jeans off. *Screw you, Michael!*

Beyond angry, I ignored the dark pit forming in my stomach. I grabbed my clean shirt and drilled it against the wall behind him. Stupid idea but I wasn't going to walk around to grab it. I threw my hands in the air as Michael watched me with ticked off eyes. Standing in my underwear and bra, I sat on the bed and leaned against the headboard, crossing my ankles as I stretched my legs out on the bed. Thank bloody-goodness I hadn't mentioned I'd gone outside, or bumping into Joshua.

He sat down on the bed and held the journal up to me, a long page of writing staring me in the face. He wasn't going to back down. He was lucky he wasn't a Grollic, I'd have gladly told him where to go. "What the hell does this say?"

"What's the matter with you?" I stared at him. "It's plain English. Read it yourself." I pointed to the door. "You know what? Just get out! Shut the door behind you and go find Rob. He'll explain how I unleashed a demon from hell."

He ignored the gravity of truth in my words and shook his head, his body stiff and unyielding as he moved further on the bed and tore the book from my fingers.

"It's not English." He growled softly and turned, picking up the wolf journal and flipping to a page before turning them both to me. "Same language. See? You didn't tell me you could write like this." He snorted, his nostrils flaring. "Were you lying all this time? Can you read Bentos' journal and you pretended you couldn't?"

I sat up and grabbed them both, the languages looking very different to me. I concentrated, trying to pull the truth from the situation around me as my heart began beating faster. If he was accusing me of this thing, then it was what he saw. Why couldn't I?

I closed my eyes and tried to settle myself, the day having been far too much already.

Reveal the truth.

Shock wouldn't cover the emotion that ran through me as the words of my personal journal shifted. I screamed and chucked both books across the room, horror washing over me. Was I turning fully Grollic? I stared at Michael. "What's happening to me?"

His face went from pure anger to confusion to something else I couldn't read. "You didn't know?"

Tears coursed down my cheeks and splashed on the bed as I shook my head. I brought my knees to my chest and buried my head into my arms.

Michael crawled to me on his knees, pulling me up and wrapping his strong arms around me.

I cried harder, so many emotions swimming in the recess of my chest and leaving me empty and beyond scared.

"How could you not know?"

"I don't know, Michael. I don't know anything right now. The wolf from earlier is following us. Joshua was on the beach. I just talked to him a few minutes ago."

"Did he hurt you?" Michael stiffened. His expression birthed another wave of fear inside of me.

"No, but I think he can force me to read Bentos' journal. I can see parts that were hidden before." I felt the cool metal of Michael's pendant press against my chest. "He showed me how to read the page with the triangle symbol. The power of three is the Siorgha, the journal and me."

He pulled me close and I sunk into his hold, my tears slowly drying. The familiar smell of him and the warmth of his embrace began to melt me. "I called Bentos here. Joshua thinks it's our best chance at stopping Bentos. We need to fight."

"You called him here?" Michael moved back again, his fingers tight on my upper arms.

I wanted to suffocate in the smell of him and pretend that happily ever after could exist and that blood and claws weren't the only future I could imagine. "A page in the journal gave me the words to summon him."

"And you could read it."

"When Joshua was near I could. Like he had the power to unlock my power. I don't know. I'm scared. I should never have gone up there without you, but you were so angry. I'm tired of hurting you or upsetting you." I sunk back against him as he moved us to lay down. He shifted and moved on top of me, my legs opening to make room for him.

"Don't go near him again. Something isn't right." He reached down and brushed the hair from my face, his eyes lighting up brightly as they moved over me. "You're beautiful, even when you're mad, or sad." His finger ran along my cheek wiping a last tear away.

"Really? I just feel like a monster." I choked on a sob that worked its way up my chest. "I feel like the monster that's going to destroy us."

"Nothing will take you from me."

"It feels like something already is," I whispered and closed my eyes, turning my head to try and ease the painful burn in my chest and throat as fresh tears dropped off my nose onto the bed. His fingers were soft as he forced me to focus on him. "What happened up there? I felt it down here."

"I think it was a surge of my power."

He grinned, as if proud of me. "Whether you called Bentos or not, that power'll bring him running. This was inevitable." He looked down, refusing to meet my gaze. "I called Caleb earlier. He's coming."

"What? No. I don't want him to take my brother." I stiffened and tried to move from underneath Michael, but he pinned me down, his lips pressing to mine as the world faded.

"I won't let him touch Rob. I promise. Trust me." He broke the kiss and whispered for me to trust him.

I wanted to. I needed to.

Reaching up, he took my arms and pulled them around his neck before pressing soft kisses along my neck until his lips touched my ear. "No matter how worried I am or how angry and lost I feel, with you in my arms the world rights itself. I'm not the enemy. I'm your mate, your forever, your love. Remember that tonight, no matter what happens."

"I love you." I leaned up and kissed him hard as he moved to hover over me again. The kiss was passionate and hungry, his hands getting lost in my long hair. I pulled at the bottom of his shirt and he moved from me, pulling it off and standing up as I watched him. He tugged his jeans off and stood before me for a second, his eyes moving down my half-clothed body. I shivered and reached for him, knowing this moment was long overdue.

He climbed back in the bed and sat back on his heels as my eyes moved across him, taking in the most intimate parts of him. He left nothing on and as I sat up, he reached behind me to undo my bra, his eyes moving down to covet me as I tossed the silky material past him. My stomach tightened when he leaned over and pressed his face softly to my stomach, breathing in deeply and growling, the sound skittering across my skin.

He looped his strong fingers into the sides of my panties and pulled down as I let out a long sigh, my mind settling to the idea that we're to be one in all things. He moved back up my body, settling himself on top of me and kissing me a few times softly before he stopped, his eyes on mine, his tone thick but serious.

"I want this. I want us to unite. I don't know what it means for the future, but I will always love you. I want this gift to be yours, to be mine."

"Yes, I want it too." I reached up and pulled him as he wrapped his arms around me and took me to heights far beyond anything power could offer.

Chapter 17

"Stay close to me tonight." Michael's arms wrapped tightly around me, as if he feared letting me go might lose me forever.

"I will. I'm scared." I tucked myself against his naked body, our lovemaking sweet and gentle – perfect. In this moment of chaos, I clung to it.

Michael leaned against the headboard. "The others are going to wonder where we are."

I smiled against his chest. "More like what you're doing to me since you've been so mad."

He absently stroked my shoulder. "Probably." The corners of his mouth turned down. "Caleb's going to be here."

And there went the mood. "I can't believe you called him without telling me."

"Really? 'Cause I can't believe you went out and spoke to *Joshua* without telling me." He raised an eyebrow and waited to see if I would argue. When I didn't respond he continued. "Caleb's coming because we're not ready. However with him and your Grollic pack beside us, we stand a fighting chance."

"Bentos is coming for me. He won't be on his own. He'll have an army with him."

"We will too. Your focus needs to be tapping into the power that lays within your DNA, Rouge." He traced a heart shape on my shoulder. "You're beyond powerful, which is going to scare all of us, but we know you can do it. I know you can."

I moved from his hold, running my fingers through the mess that was my hair and kneeling on the floor to pick up the wolf journal. "I'm not so sure I'm ready... not sure I want to read the rest of this."

Michael shifted to his elbow, the motion causing his muscles to flex. I don't ever remember seeing someone so beautiful and sensual in my whole life as I looked back at him. Sharing myself with him had left a feeling of unity, of wholeness that belonged to soul mates. Maybe he was mine. Maybe we could find a way around this thing that sat heavy between us.

"It's not just a journal, but it belongs to you, Rouge. Not Bentos. It's yours now." He got up on the other side of the bed and walked around to me a few minutes later, my clothes gathered in his hands as he pulled me up, his jeans on, his smile wide and reaching his eyes.

"Get dressed and let's go find the others. We have lots to do."

He kissed me and turned to move as I stopped him, pulling him back as he chuckled. It was a lovely sound and it warmed me in ways nothing else could. I missed the sound.

"Keep an eye on that spell book of yours."

Spells? "Only witches can read incantations."

"You don't think you have a witch-like power? After everything?" He chuckled and kissed my nose and shook his head as he moved from me, leaning over and picking up his shirt. He pulled it over his head and looked back at me. "You just continue to become more and more complex, don't you?"

"I'm not a witch."

He gave a low laugh. "You should probably rethink that. I'll meet you down there."

"I love you."

"Me too." He winked and walked from the room as I stood and laid the journal on the bed in front of me. I pulled on various pieces of clothing and tried to think through his words. I was Grollic and I was the seventh child of the seventh son. Power was inherent, but being a witch on top of that? How was that even possible? Being the seventh made me something like a witch, but not some Voodoo kind. Just one who could control Grollics?

I hurried quickly down the hall, my feet still bare, and my hair now in a messy ponytail. The sound of everyone speaking in solemn tones didn't forebode well, but I knew it was a night that would set the future right. I just didn't want any bodies left lying on the beach to be anyone in this place.

Everyone stopped talking and glanced my way as I walked in. A soft smile on Grace's lips let me know she wasn't mad at me anymore. Her eyes shifted to Michael and then back to me, her brows wagging. *She knows.*

Michael stood and moved toward me, sliding his hand into mine and moving so we could sit together at the table.

"You've already talked to them?" I asked Michael. My voice was steady, but held no accusations.

"No, I did," Rob spoke before crossing his arms over his strong chest. "We need to know how this is going to go down."

Grace sat beside my brother, a little too close for casual friends.

"Joshua's bringing the pack from yesterday." I nibbled at the cheese, the rich flavor welcomed as it spread across my tongue.

"The one that tried to attack us?" Seth asked.

"They were testing us." Michael took a turn. "They were seeing if Rouge was who she was supposed to be. I didn't know it then, but I'm assured of it now. When she turned and froze that massive group of Grollics in their place, the Alpha knew he had found her."

"Caleb's coming too?" Seth shook his head. "He's not going to fight with Grollics."

"He will if I control them." I glanced at Rob, not missing the uncertainty in his eyes. "Everyone here has to agree to protect Rob. Caleb will not touch him."

The fight would be epic and we needed to pull together if we even wanted to make a dent in this situation before us. However, no one was going to touch my brother. If Caleb attempted it while I was fighting Bentos, I'd find a way to kill the immortal original myself by sending every Grollic there to bite him.

I had the power of three with me. The darkness of that power couldn't have me, nor would Caleb. I was loved by an angel and wrapped in trust and rightness by my friends and a new brother. I was going to make this right.

Rob glanced up and winked at me before turning back to the table and laughing loudly, Seth having said something I'd missed. Michael slipped his hand into mine and leaned over to kiss my cheek.

"You okay?" He reached up and brushed his fingers past my cheek.

"Yeah, I think so. For the first time in a long time I think so."

"Good." He leaned over and kissed me again, the deep voice from the door causing him to jerk back as if slapped.

"What are you doing here? Laughing at a table? Why aren't you preparing weapons, getting ready to attack?" Caleb stepped into the room, his eyes moving across everyone and narrowing in on me. "Sounds like you've made a right mess."

"I'm about to clean it up." I didn't want to appear rude, but no way was I letting Michael's mentor intimidate me ever again.

Caleb shifted his eyes toward Rob, the truth of his knowing Rob was a Grollic washing over his regal features. A hiss escaped his lips before he turned to Michael. "A word." He turned and walked out as Michael stood up, no expression on his handsome face.

"Start heading up to the surface. We'll be there shortly," Michael spoke before he left the room, his voice never wavering.

"I'm assuming that was your father?" Rob looked toward Grace as he reached out and took her hand. "I should have introduced myself."

Grace pulled her hand out of his and hit him on the back of the head. "Idiot." She didn't sound like she meant it. "He's actually more like a guardian."

"We need to get going. Finish up." Seth straightened, his face a mask of what was to come.

I followed him and headed down the hall.

I could hear Caleb and Michael yelling at one another. I wanted to keep walking, but I couldn't. I knew how much Caleb despised Michael and I being together. I was just a pawn in his game.

"What the hell happened here? That girl is dangerous. You'd better wake up and get your head on straight."

"She's learning to control it."

"And then what? She's one of them!"

"She has my Siorgha."

Caleb hissed. "I love lots of things, but if I found myself in love with a poisonous snake then I would seek help. You figure this out. We are Hunters and were brought here to fight the Grollics. Your purpose has once again become skewed. She will be the one that kills you. You're going to need to decide what side you are on – theirs, or ours." Something banged against the wall close to where I stood. "And then you go and bring a Grollic into my house?"

"We fight tonight." Michael's voice grated like nails on a chalkboard. "I'm not having this conversation with you right now, Caleb. We could have Bentos in our hands tonight and close this down."

"It isn't settled until Rouge's power is squelched. Bentos is only one of two threats, Michael."

"Don't force me to choose right now. I wouldn't choose in a manner that would leave you proud."

"I'm sad to hear that." Caleb's voice moved closer to the door, warning me I needed to get out of the way. "Tonight we fight, but you pay close attention to her. She's a ticking time bomb and when she goes off, it'll be you that I send after her to shut her down... for good."

I walked quickly past the mostly closed door and slipped into my room, my heart aching for the situation I had once again put Michael in. Now wasn't the time to think about it and I knew without a doubt that Michael wouldn't let Caleb do anything to me during the fight.

Now I had to focus on making sure I didn't appear to be this all-powerful, black magic witch as I fought against a villain that begged me to be just that.

What if there was a choice to make?

Become that darkness for the night to save my friends and close down this never-ending struggle, but lose Michael in the process. Or play it safe and watch everyone I love fall underneath the foot of the tyrant that wanted me dead?

I knew one thing for sure. I wanted this over – for good. I would be compelled to do whatever it took.

Chapter 18

"It's time." Michael's voice startled me as I looked up from the wolf journal. So many answers revealed and yet so many to go. I tucked it in the back of my jeans and reached to pull my hair into a less messy ponytail as he watched me. The slight tick at the side of his eye let me know more about his internal thoughts than he would ever care to share.

"I'm ready." I walked toward him, my voice strong and sure. I reached up and brushed my hand over the necklace, the power of three with me. I would defeat Bentos or die trying tonight.

Michael pulled me against him, his arms locking around my waist.

"Whatever happens tonight, I love you."

"I love you too." I leaned up and pressed my lips to his, wanting so badly to ask if love was enough, but I couldn't. I knew the answer. He would believe it to be, but it wasn't. If we got through the night before us, another battle was on the horizon, one that wouldn't split flesh and spill blood, but one that would separate family from family and mate from mate.

A Hunter and a Grollic weren't meant to be. I was the Seventh Mark, power incarnate for my lot in life and condemnation my prize.

I reluctantly released him and walked toward the elevator, looking for the others.

"They're already on the surface level. I was just up there as well."

How long had I been reading the journal? "Have the Grollics gathered?"

I moved into the elevator and leaned forward to hold the door for him. He nodded and moved to stand beside me, his arm brushing mine. There were a million things I wanted to say and I'm sure he had a million of his own as well. Neither of us spoke a word on the quick ride up.

I stepped from the elevator and headed toward my brother, Rob standing and talking with Joshua as if they were familiar. I looked over my shoulder to see Caleb talking intently with Seth and Grace. My prayer for the night was that we wouldn't remain divided, but come together to make this go the way it needed to.

I smelled the air and closed my eyes, trying to see if I could sense Bentos' approach.

"There you are. How are you holding up?" Joshua moved toward me, reaching for me and pulling me into a hug as he pressed the top of his chin to my head. Peace washed over me at a staggering rate. I needed to remain close to him during the fight... just to keep my calm. It would deter Michael, but trying to explain it would only cause a wedge between us. Why did I only feel the pull to Joshua when he was around? I pushed the thought aside as Michael frowned in our direction and slipped my arm around Rob, making it appear as though I was just shifting to love on my brother.

The questioning look Rob gave me and the words he spoke were lost in the sound of the wind picking up. I turned and looked out behind us. There had to be more than two hundred Grollics standing ready.

"You're the Alpha of a pack this large?" Rob sounded impressed.

"Yes, and I'm tired of turning power over to a villain." Joshua watched his beasts with pride.

"I know. I am too." Rob rolled his shoulder and cracked his neck.

"He's going to bring his own army. You need to prepare." I looked toward the boys next to me.

"It'd better be a mighty army then."

No sooner had he spoken that the ground under my feet trembled. I took a step forward to keep myself from taking several back. The Hunters moved to stand beside me, Michael reaching for my hand.

"We do this together," he whispered, his brow tightening as he looked past me.

"Yeah, we do," Joshua responded and stepped up to the other side of me, slipping his hand into mine as well. My passion stood on my left and my peace on my right.

I didn't get a chance to respond as the sound of the massive army of beasts coming over the edge of the thin forest a hundred yards from us was like a sea of black.

"There are too many of them," Caleb spoke and moved to stand in front of all of us.

"No. I can handle them, just pick off the really strong ones." I released myself from Joshua and Michael and raced toward the oncoming war, my hands held out in front of me.

"Rouge, where are you going?" Michael yelled above the roar of their stampeding hooves. I looked back and smiled, my eyes only seeing through the dark haze of power that pulsed through me.

Bentos appeared in the middle of the men, near the front line.

He walked toward us, his head held high, the smile on his lips brilliant. He was a replica of me, his dark copper hair silky and highlighted in its natural hue. His amber eyes lit as if small fireflies danced behind his gaze.

I skidded to a stop a healthy distance from him and steeled my resolve, the battle cry of the beasts behind him way outdoing my own army. He wasn't tall, or muscular. There was nothing in his physical attributes that screamed power. However, the strength behind his eyes that were filled with hatred terrified me to the bone.

"Jamie... finally we meet. I've been looking for you." He smiled as if amused. "I even considered you might be dead, at one point."

"That's not happening tonight."

"Your death?" He laughed, which sounded like a sneer to me. "It's you I want."

"That's not going to happen." If I died then he would take what little power I have and lay waste to all I love. I glanced over my shoulder, the pensive stares burning me with anger as they waited.

"I see you've brought the twins, and the bastard."

"Who's the bastard?" I turned and reached behind me, brushing my fingers along the book, but unwilling to pull it out. If he knew I had it, all would be lost. Not until the proper time.

"Of course not. A Grollic is not to be mated to a Hunter. What a loss of power. Do you not know that an intermingled child would be born and you would bastardize the great gift you've been given?"

I swallowed my questions for another time. I had made love to Michael. What did that mean? What validity did that even give his words? I worked through my mind to pull the power of three together. I needed to feel the warmth of the journal and the chill of the necklace to know that I was right.

"Joshua, is that you?" he called out, barely raising his voice. For a man as old as Caleb, he didn't age. Did I have that same ability? Bentos turned his attention to me and tsked as he shook his head. "He's the greatest Alpha of the Grollics. He stands beside you and defies me?" Bentos laughed loudly, the sound physically stinging me.

I stifled a shudder and readied myself. "I have the power of three on my side. You'll not win this."

"Me winning would be taking you with me."

"To kill me slowly another time?"

"To train you to be the monster you were born to be."

"Never! I would never go with you anywhere." Evil, dark power emanated from him.

"It's inevitable. You will become darkness with or without me."

I swallowed hard. There was no way I would go with him.

He moved faster than I thought possible, spinning me and tightening his arms around my upper torso as I spun to watch the horrified faces of my friends. "Dear Michael, do you wish to see the same thing happen to her as it happened to your sister?" He laughed and held me, a blade appearing in his hand.

Michael let out a cry that shook the clouds in heaven. They charged toward me, the Hunters so fast, but not fast enough. Bentos spoke to the beasts and forced them to attack. The Grollics behind charged, rushing forward. I tried to pull from him, but his arms were like steel.

"Were you not out of control when you stole your brother's ability to transform? How about when you hurt him in your anger, froze him with your rage, crippled him with your indifference?" He laughed as I pulled harder. "And those Grollics out West? Did you think I don't know what you're capable of? That I wouldn't find out?"

I screamed in rage as the ground beneath me shook hard. With a strong jerk I pulled from him and turned to face him. "I can control myself."

"Caleb seems to think so too. Don't you know that when this is over they will hunt someone new, fresh... a danger to society?"

"You're wrong."

"Am I, *daughter*?" With a flick of his wrist, more Grollics appeared and raced toward Michael and everyone around him. Joshua seemed to be controlling his pack and held their ground.

I drew a line on the beach. "This is where you stand. By tomorrow you'll be dead."

I turned to race to the fight but Bentos caught my arm.

I spun and pulled it from him, summoning power from deep inside of me. "I call the power of three." I felt a jolt of electricity hit the inside of my chest and I lifted my arms.

"You cannot defeat me, Rouge. You have yet to earn the triune power. I can teach you though. Come with me. No one else will train you and raise you to know who you are and where you come from."

My hands lifted into the air as I screamed 'No' over and over. The wolves around me dropped in place, the sound of them hitting the ground almost deafening as they screamed in pain. I turned in horror as darkness pressed in all around me. Now was my chance.

I turned back to Bentos and lifted my hands toward him. "I take from you all the power that you hold. It is now to be mine and you... you can rest in peace and leave us be."

He lifted his hand and turned it slightly, the pinch in my chest starting out small and gaining as I hit my knees. My ability to use my gifts failed me in the moment I needed them most.

"Rouge!" I heard Michael holler as I pressed my hands to the earth, the air so thick and difficult to breathe. What had I thought? I would fight the most powerful Grollic in the world and not fall before him? I was a child where he was concerned... a dead one at that. I fought to stay conscious.

"Stop Hunter or I'll squeeze the last bit of her life from her lungs," Bentos growled, the sound of it alone sending terror rushing through me. A set of Grollics surrounded Michael, their teeth bared and the poison dripping from their mouths.

I reached out in front of me as a light began to grow, the hold on my heart weakening as it grew brighter. Was I creating it? I pressed my cheek to the coolness of the ground beneath me as my eyes blurred. The Grollics were rising again, my ability to keep them down gone as I lay struggling to not succumb to the grip Bentos had on my heart.

"You're as useless as the others," Bentos hissed, his words full of venom. "I should've known better than to think you worthy. I waited this long for you to rise and for what? A fist fight not even worth my time."

The grip he held on me tightened. I tried to fight it. He would kill me and everyone here. How could I have been so stupid to think we stood a chance against him? His face burned an image behind my eyelids. He showed me what he was going to do to Grace, to Rob, to Michael. I broke and cried out, reaching for the light in front of me. "Help... me," I whispered hoarsely.

"You cannot have her!" A woman's voice rang loud and radiated around me as if she were screaming just above my head.

I rolled over to my side as Joshua moved in and picked me up, his arms strong, his body offering peace as I gasped for air and tried to tell my heart not to give out while trying to find where the voice came from. It didn't take long. A stunning, beautiful woman dressed full in creamy white leather, with a flowing jacket, or cape—I couldn't tell—stood with her hand out, as if protecting me from Bentos.

"She's not yours for the taking!" She glared at him, the anger in her face terrifying. "You control and dictate those around you, but you cannot have her!" She lunged forward and shoved Bentos with a strength I'd never seen before.

Bentos flew backwards and landed on the ground with a thump that shook the earth. He shrieked and called the beasts around him to attack her. They immediately pounced.

I screamed in horror. Whoever this strange woman was, I didn't want her to die. I fought to break free of Joshua's hold, but he held me tight.

"You're not ready. Gain your strength," he instructed. "Use your words."

She held them off. Fighting and killing like it was a dance. Her cape flew around behind her as she spun, shifted and lunged. It reminded me of Caleb in a way.

While she fought, the others joined in to help her. Caleb, Michael, Grace, Seth, they all moved as if joining the dance. Rob must have shifted as I couldn't see him.

I closed my eyes and began to chant, like I was begging. "Stop! I tell you to stop fighting! Shift back. Lay down your weapons. Leave us alone. Go away. Run far, far away. Don't let Bentos control you. Break the hold he has on you. Run. Spend your life running from that monster. Stop fighting." My voice rose as I gasped for breath. I had no idea if it worked.

The deafening sound grew quieter, but my powerful ability wasn't enough to stop Bentos. I continued saying anything that would help us. Bentos' words held more strength than mine did. For every command I called out, he countered with his own.

Terrible cries and shrieks of death filled the air. Bentos' men continued coming at us in droves. Every Hunter fought alongside three or four Grollics Joshua had brought.

The strange woman had to be a Hunter. She fought like them, and yet completely different. She pressed hard, working her way to the center of a pack protecting Bentos. She forced him back to the edge of the property. Grollics began disappearing back into the tree line from which they had come. They knew they were losing. Fight or flight took over whatever Bentos and I could command.

Bentos stood glaring at her and then me. Four or five Grollics stood by his side. He jumped onto the back of the largest one and spoke into its ear. I couldn't hear what he said from the distance apart. The beast swung around and took off into the forest.

The woman, her white outfit covered in blood, turned around quickly. She smiled at me and stroked the Grollic who had been fighting alongside her. *Rob?* She lifted her fingers to her lips and blew me a kiss before disappearing into the forest after Bentos.

"Who the hell was that?" Michael raced over to me as Joshua put me down on the ground. Michael pulled me into his arms.

He was covered in blood but I didn't care, as long as none of it was his own.

"That," Rob said as he walked up to us, clearly naked after shifting back from Grollic to human form. He winked at Grace, who pulled something out of the small backpack she had on. Rob slipped on the shorts she had tossed him. "Was mother." He scanned the forest, as if expecting her to reappear any moment.

"Rebekah was your mother?" Caleb asked, his question directed to me.

"I don't know." I clung to Michael, the world still unsteady.

"She is." Rob turned as a tear dripped down his face. "She died. I buried her... how?"

"She's a Hunter!" Caleb stared at me, his face masked in anger. "Dammit!" he shouted and walked off.

"Rebekah's a Hunter?" Rob asked, racing to catch up with Caleb as Grace ran after them both.

If the world didn't seem crazy enough, it had just doubled in its complexity. "What does that mean for me?" I looked up at Michael hoping he had the answer.

"I don't know." Michael's mouth moved into a tight line. "Stay here with Joshua. I need to talk to Caleb."

"This battle is over for tonight." Joshua reached for me.

I leaned toward the stranger who I felt like I'd known all my life. Weariness sat heavy on my shoulders. "Yes... but I think we've just started the war."

Chapter 19

I could hear them arguing in the room next to me, my heart breaking at the fight Michael was putting up. Bentos had been right. I was next on their list. I was no longer a simple girl or even a Grollic. I was the seventh child of the seventh son and my mother was a Huntress. I had slept with Michael and broken the rules that govern us all. I pulled my bag from the ground as Caleb's voice ripped through the room next to me, his demands clear.

"She's not staying here, Michael! This has gone too far." Something shattered against the wall. "She leaves, now!"

"I'm going too," Michael yelled in response.

"No you're not! You're taking Seth and Grace and following Bentos. This isn't a game that we're hoping to win. It's a war. Start acting like it."

"I know this is a war!" I imagined Michael standing, his feet spread and his hands on his hips.

"Get your Siorgha from her! She's an abomination! I won't ask you to do it again, but don't you dare ask me not to."

"I hate you. I'm no longer part of this." Michael's voice was almost too soft to hear, but the hatred was clear.

I hurried to gather my things, tears dripping from my cheeks and rolling down my chin. I shoved my clothes into a bag. "I don't want to do this." New tears sprung as I reached around my neck and unclasped the chain. I held the beautiful pendant, Michael's blood, his heartbeat lay inside the centre. Sighing, I gently laid it on the bed where he would see it before running toward the door. I didn't have much time. Caleb wanted me dead and Michael would die trying to protect me.

Nobody was safe.

I would go after Bentos this time, power of three be damned. I could figure this out and when I destroyed him, I'd show Caleb. Prove to him I wasn't evil.

They began to argue again, the fight getting physical from the sounds of things crashing and breaking. I paused to rip a piece of paper from the journal in my hand and fumbled for a pen in the bottom of my bag.

I wrote a quick note and left it on the bed before racing toward the elevator.

"Please have Rob upstairs... Please." I had no idea where Grace or Seth were. Neither did I know about Rob. I knew Joshua had stayed near the trees when Caleb had told Michael to get into the elevator earlier.

I couldn't contain the small sobs that leaked from my lips, my heart shattering over and over again in my chest. My actions had led to this moment. All of them from that damn graveyard to pulling the darkest power available to me during the fight.

It was quiet when the elevator door slid open. I glanced into the night sky, my eyes adjusting instantly.

Joshua and Rob stood talking off near the beach, the rest of the pack gone. They looked my way as I ran frantically to them.

"We have to go." I didn't try to hide my tears.

"Go where?" Rob moved up and tried to slow me. He held me, his face full of confusion. "Your eyes. They look blue."

I pushed past him as I continued to run toward the forest. "It's probably just the night sky reflecting blue."

"Jamie, where are you going?"

"Caleb's going to kill me. We have to go," I screamed behind me, the realization that Michael might have to give up his life to save me propelling me forward.

"Does Michael know you're leaving?" Rob caught up to me as Joshua ran past us.

"Not at this exact moment, but he will. There isn't much he can do about it. Caleb won't let him go."

We ran through the forest, following Joshua as he veered to the right. A small black truck sat half hidden in the forest. Joshua pulled keys out and unlocked the door. He jumped behind the steering wheel and started the engine.

We pulled out and headed for the road to take us out of the forest, to a road and then on to the highway. Joshua reached over and touched my hand, pulling it to his lips and kissing my fingers. "I only wanted to keep us safe."

I watched the world go by as tears continued to drop down my cheeks.

"It's better this way, Jamie. We are your people. I'm your mate."

I turned and let my eyes move across Joshua's face as he glanced toward me. "I know." I straightened and faced forward, hardening my emotions, trying to shut them off. "First we find Bentos. Then we'll find Rebekah. I have some questions I want to ask her."

Rob reached up and rubbed my shoulder. "So do I. So do I."

I pictured the Siorgha laying lost on the bed. My note to Michael beside it.

I love you in this life and the next, but Fate's Intent was never to see us together. I'm with my people now. I'll right this thing with Bentos for us... for you. Goodbye, Michael.

~ Rouge

~ THE END ~

FATE'S INTERVENTION
Bk 5 in the Hidden Secrets Saga

Note from the Author;

I hope you enjoyed reading Compelled. I'm so excited to be able to continue this series!

If you have a moment to post a review to let others know about the story, I would greatly appreciate it! I love hearing from my fans so feel free to send me a message on Facebook or by email so we can chat.

All the best, W.J. May

Hidden Secrets Saga:

Download Seventh Mark part 1 For FREE
Seventh Mark part 2
Marked by Destiny
Compelled
Fate's Intervention
Chosen Three
Book Trailer:
http://www.youtube.com/watch?v=Y-_vVYC1gvo

W.J. May Info:

Website: http://www.wanitamay.yolasite.com
Facebook: https://www.facebook.com/pages/Author-WJ-May-FAN-PAGE/141170442608149
SIGN UP FOR **W.J. May's Newsletter** to find out about new releases, updates, cover reveals and even freebies!
http://eepurl.com/97aYf

More from W.J. May

THE CHRONICLES OF KERRIGAN

Rae of Hope is FREE!

Book Trailer:
http://www.youtube.com/watch?v=gILAwXxx8MU

BOOK BLURB:

How hard do you have to shake the family tree to find the truth about the past?

Fifteen year-old Rae Kerrigan never really knew her family's history. Her mother and father died when she was young and it is only when she accepts a scholarship to the prestigious Guilder Boarding School in England that a mysterious family secret is revealed.

Will the sins of the father be the sins of the daughter?

As Rae struggles with new friends, a new school and a star-struck forbidden love, she must also face the ultimate challenge: receive a tattoo on her sixteenth birthday with specific powers that may bind her to an unspeakable darkness. It's up to Rae to undo the dark evil in her family's past and have a ray of hope for her future.

Victoria: Daughter of Darkness
Book 1 is Free
Description:

Only Death Could Stop Her Now

The Daughters of Darkness is a series of female heroines who may or may not know each other, but all have the same father, Vlad Montour.

Victoria is a Hunter Vampire, one of the last of her kind. She's the best of the best.

When she finds out one of her marks is actually her sister she lets her go, only to end up on the wrong side of the council.

Forced to prove herself she hunts her next mark, a werewolf. Injured and hungry, she is forced to do what she must to survive. Her actions upset the ancient council and she finds herself now being the one thing she has always despised – the Hunted.

This is Tori's story by W.J. May. This is a novella. As a courtesy, the author wishes to inform you this novella does end with a cliffhanger.

RADIUM HALOS – THE SENSELESS SERIES
Book 1 is FREE:

Book Blurb:

Everyone needs to be a hero at one point in their life.

The small town of Elliot Lake will never be the same again.

Caught in a sudden thunderstorm, Zoe, a high school senior from Elliot Lake, and five of her friends take shelter in an abandoned uranium mine. Over the next few days, Zoe's hearing sharpens drastically, beyond what any normal human being can detect. She tells her friends, only to learn that four others have an increased sense as well. Only Kieran, the new boy from Scotland, isn't affected.

Fashioning themselves into superheroes, the group tries to stop the strange occurrences happening in their little town. Muggings, break-ins, disappearances, and murder begin to hit too close to home. It leads the team to think someone knows about their secret – someone who wants them all dead.

An incredulous group of heroes. A traitor in the midst. Some dreams are written in blood.

Book 1 is FREE
Book Blurb:

What if courage was your only option?

When Kallie lands a college interview with the city's new hot-shot police officer, she has no idea everything in her life is about to change. The detective is young, handsome and seems to have an unnatural ability to stop the increasing local crime rate. Detective Liam's particular interest in Kallie sends her heart and head stumbling over each other.

When a raging blood feud between vampires spills into her home, Kallie gets caught in the middle. Torn between love and family loyalty she must find the courage to fight what she fears the most and possibly risk everything, even if it means dying for those she loves.

Shadow of Doubt

Part 1 is FREE!

Book Trailer:

http://www.youtube.com/watch?v=LZK09Fe7kgA

Book Blurb:

What happens when you fall for the one you are forbidden to love?

Erebus is a bit of a lost soul. He's a guy so he should be out to have fun but unlike the rest of his kind, he is solemn and withdrawn. That is, until he meets Aurora, a law student at Cornell University. His entire world is shaken. Feelings he's never had and urges he's never understood take over. These strange longings drive him to question everything about himself

When a jealous ex stalks back into his life, he must decide if he is willing to risk everything to be with Aurora. His desire for her could destroy her, or worse, erase his own existence forever.

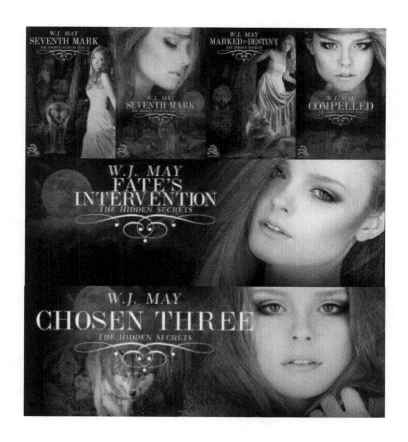

Don't miss out!

Click the button below and you can sign up to receive emails whenever W.J. May publishes a new book. There's no charge and no obligation.

Did you love *Compelled*? Then you should read *Ancient Blood of the Vampire and Werewolf* by W.J. May et al.!

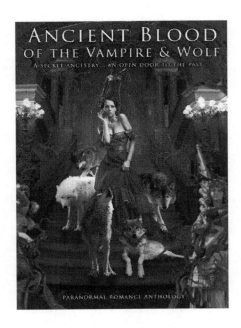

A Secret Ancestry... An Open Door to the Past.

7 Fantastic Vampire & Werewolf Shifter Stories from today's best-selling authors,

All in One ANTHOLOGY!

VAMPIRE IN DENIAL by Dale Meyers
BOOK 4
ONCE BITTEN By Trina M Lee
BOOK 5
VENOM By Kristen Middleton
BOOK 6
RESOUNDING TRUTH by Kate Thomas
BOOK 7
SEVENTH MARK – Part 1 by W.J. May

A Paranormal Romance Anthology
* Note: Some of these first in a series may be in a cliff hanger *

Also by W.J. May

Bit-Lit Series
Lost Vampire
Cost of Blood
Price of Death

Blood Red Series
Courage Runs Red
The Night Watch
Marked by Courage
Forever Night

Daughters of Darkness: Victoria's Journey
Victoria
Huntress
Coveted (A Vampire & Paranormal Romance)
Twisted

Hidden Secrets Saga
Seventh Mark - Part 1
Seventh Mark - Part 2
Marked By Destiny
Compelled
Fate's Intervention
Chosen Three

The Chronicles of Kerrigan
Rae of Hope
Dark Nebula
House of Cards

Royal Tea
Under Fire
End in Sight
Hidden Darkness
Twisted Together
Mark of Fate
Strength & Power
Last One Standing
Rae of Light

The Chronicles of Kerrigan Prequel
Christmas Before the Magic
Question the Darkness
Into the Darkness

The Hidden Secrets Saga
Seventh Mark (part 1 & 2)

The Senseless Series
Radium Halos
Radium Halos - Part 2
Nonsense

The X Files
Code X
Replica X

Standalone
Shadow of Doubt (Part 1 & 2)
Five Shades of Fantasy
Glow - A Young Adult Fantasy Sampler
Shadow of Doubt - Part 2
Four and a Half Shades of Fantasy
Full Moon

Dream Fighter
What Creeps in the Night
Forest of the Forbidden
HuNted
Arcane Forest: A Fantasy Anthology
Ancient Blood of the Vampire and Werewolf

Made in the USA
Middletown, DE
22 April 2017